When Two Souls Connect

THE REAL SOUL MATE STORY

by

Steve Gunn

Edited by Johnette Duff

PublishAmerica
Baltimore

ISBN: 1-4241-1506-X
PUBLISHED BY PUBLISHAMERICA, LLLP
www.publishamerica.com
Baltimore

Printed in the United States of America

To Sarah and Sean

A huge thank you to all who contributed their stories and experiences and to everyone who I've had the pleasure to work with on their personal soul mate experiences.

Without all you this book wouldn't have been possible.

Biographies

Steve Gunn is an internationally acclaimed psychic and healer whose own soul mate experience changed his life on every level and led him on a quest to find answers to this profound and confusing phenomenon.

His research, along with the practical experience of reading, healing and counseling hundreds of soul mate cases, led him to develop in-depth theories and practical solutions, including healing techniques and meditations he calls Natural Energy Therapies, proven to alleviate pain and suffering and bring clarity in these situations.

His belief is that there is a great need for a practical, easily understood work on soul mates and associated phenomenon and his hope is that such a book can spare readers even a modicum of the pain these links can cause.

Born in Britain, Steve now lives in Florida and can be contacted via his website http://www.stevegunn.net

Johnette Duff is an attorney and a nationally-published author who has been featured on *Today* and *Good Morning America*. Although legal issues in relationships are her expertise (www.loveandthelaw.com), a recent soul mate connection wreaked havoc on what she thought she knew.

Her own quest for answers led her to Steve Gunn—his theories, tempered by his own experiences, shed light on a relationship that, as he often hears, "makes no sense." As she was gently guided to an understanding of the forces beyond her control and the knowledge that her arms were too short to box with God, she knew she wanted to share the same healing, understanding and acceptance she discovered with others still seeking their own answers.

Foreword

This book came about from an event that changed my life.

Meeting someone with whom I connected on an utterly staggering level caused a chain of events that saw a change of job, home, finances and, most importantly, changes in myself and my beliefs at the innermost levels—all of which were totally out of my control.

As I write this book, I look back and realize that I'm now a totally different person. My journey took me through levels of love and pain that I didn't even realize existed. Many times I didn't want to carry on and, through most of it, I just couldn't understand what was happening or why.

But I did emerge. Stronger, more centered and with a realization that the most important thing is the universe is love. As material as we may be, love is a force that can change anything and everything and it did. It saw me lose my fear, and come to understand myself, the universe and, I believe, the meaning of life.

Although psychic from an early age, my spiritual journey took me to previously unexplored levels of ability and healing powers. My quest for understanding led me through an intense period of study and allowed me to meet and help, as well as learn from, some wonderful and amazing people, all of whom were or had been in the same situation I found myself.

One of those people is Johnette Duff, who edited the book and contributed her own experiences.

In those early days, I vowed that when I had a full understanding of this most incredible and life changing phenomenon, I would do whatever I could to share that knowledge. Since meeting Johnette, it seemed natural to share our experiences in the hope that we can ease other's pain and help them realize what's happening in their lives. If we can accomplish that, then our experiences will have been even more worthwhile.

Steve Gunn—Surrey, England—August 2004

Chapter 1

Soul Shock

The human heart feels things the eyes cannot see, and knows what the mind cannot understand.—Robert Vallett

If you've met someone who's changed you forever…

If you love someone so much you realize you just weren't alive before them…

If you've met someone who's awakened you to the unbelievable beauty of existence…

If you've met someone who is more you than even you are…

If you miss someone so much you can't even conceive of existing without them…

If you've lost someone and it feels like your soul left with them…

then read on…

Typical of many cases I deal with is the story of Fiona and Robert.

I first met Fiona when she booked a psychic reading via telephone and I realized she was suffering a great deal of pain and confusion from the recent breakup of her relationship with Robert. I recommended she seek healing and, a week later, she arrived at my door.

I wish I had a cent for every tear that has been shed on that end of my sofa—it's a wonder it isn't afloat by now. Seeing people in complete despair is a common occurrence for me but it never gets any easier watching someone fall apart, not least because I've been there. Some days, you just wonder what the human race is coming to when people can hurt others in the way this girl was hurting. However, she was here now and I was going to help her.

Her total devastation and confusion was apparent as she sat and wept uncontrollably while she related her story, of her and Robert's meeting and falling deeply and profoundly in love, love on a level she had never previously experienced, and then right in the midst of the relationship of her dreams Robert had turned tail and run without warning.

To add to her grief and despair, within a week he had hooked up with someone else and told her he wasn't coming back.

This girl was in a total mess of pain, despair and confusion she was desperately trying to understand how this magical union had turned into a nightmare and how the man she knew without doubt to be her 'one', her life partner, could turn through 180 degrees and wound her so deeply, at the same time trashing everything she believed to be so sacred about their bond.

As I psychically read both her energies and Robert's, I realized this was a very strong connection, hence the level of suffering she was enduring. Soul mates on this level are just that…souls that are connected…an energy connection between the two souls that's just as real and just as strong as an electrical cord between them.

Fiona had been through all the stages of trying to get over him, her friends saying all the "right" things about him not being worthy of her and trying to get her to consider dating other men but it hadn't worked. And this is what a soul mate union is all about. It doesn't work and it can't. 'Moving on' or 'getting over it' is something that is just not possible, certainly not until years into the future and in many cases never…

The domain of true soul mates is the domain of the metaphysical practitioner. By that I mean psychics, mediums and healers like myself. People usually come to us because nothing else makes sense and nothing else works. A soul mate connection can only be understood at the soul level, the level of the connection itself, why it happened, what it's meant to achieve and how it affects both parties.

However much love, caring and counseling the person gets it is usually startlingly ineffective in consoling people experiencing what Fiona was experiencing. This is one of the ways we first identify a soul connection, by the fact that strong, accomplished, sensible people just totally fall to pieces and just can't get over what's happened.

Psychics like myself 'read' soul or spiritual energy, that's how we know what people are feeling and thinking, what their characters are like, what makes them tick, how they work and even what they look like. We also read the 'cosmic' energy, that is, destiny's part in the scheme of things and what's meant to happen and usually what will happen and more importantly why.

By tuning into Robert's energies in the usual way I knew he was in love with her. Fiona, however, was in no position to believe this, not based on his actions. It was totally clear to me, however, that the bond between them was strong and had grown ever stronger and stronger whilst they were together, to the point that it scared the hell out of Robert.

The link between them was so incredibly 'meant to be' that it had destiny stamped all over it. So how do you tell someone that a person they love has hurt them because they love them too much?

How do you explain that the 'runner' fears the intensity of the connection? I could tell this other woman meant nothing to Robert and was just a shoulder for him to cry on. But, to Fiona, it seemed he had been a cheater and had callously lied about loving her. That's a very natural assumption when someone you trust totally turns a one eighty and goes off with someone else without warning.

For those of us who are emotionally and spiritually open to love on any level, the idea of someone running from happiness is bizarre and cruel in the extreme. Fiona was struggling to make sense of it and wasn't winning at all, which added to her immense grief.

It's important to understand that high-level connections like this one are so profound and so deep that they change your very consciousness, your innermost emotions and even your understanding of who you are. They are all consuming and utterly transformational and it's feeling the awesome power of that transformation and having no choice no brakes, no control whatsoever that usually scares the heck out of one of the partners.

As I began Fiona's healing and looked at what had happened to her energies, I realized she was suffering from what I call 'soul shock.' When someone you have a deep connection with suddenly pulls away, the disconnect leaves you feeling as if your soul has left your body, like an empty shell. You just can't get back to reality and you can feel as if you simply exist.

This experience is similar to grieving the death of a loved one and I know many counselors, at least those who accept and understand connections, who will treat this pain in the same way as bereavement.

Even after more cases than I can remember, it never fails to amaze me how powerful healing is and what a perfect tool it can be for dealing with soul mate connections. Although what's loosely known as spiritual healing can seem mysterious and bizarre it's concept is simple once you accept that all souls are energy—as psychics we can 'read' that energy—and as healers we can manipulate the energy. The 'how' is not within the scope of the book however a later chapter goes into more detail of how soul mate connections work at the energy level.

So using healing, I was able to intervene in Fiona's energies and their link to Robert to give her some peace and a change to start to at least function again. The process is pulling Robert's energy away from Fiona's so that she wasn't being tugged around like a leaf in a gale by his confusion.

Unexpressed emotions are debilitating and dangerous, so I used a technique I call 'accelerated bereavement.' This acceleration brings out the despair and pain in a burst of crying that's so deep you know it's from the soul. But, after twenty minutes or so, this incredible pain eases and the subject calms. That's exactly what happened with Fiona.

What is unique about soul connections is that we feel our partner's grief and confusion and they feel ours—remember the connection is real in every way and links both partners emotions and senses. This creates a tsunami of pain as the emotions flow both ways across our spiritual link and bounces each of us around like two corks on a string. Using healing energy to put a block in a place eases 'soul shock' tremendously, so that's what I did to allow Fiona a chance to get on her feet again.

As the weeks and months went by, I saw her and treated her on a regular basis. Throughout that time, she grew slowly but progressively stronger, even as she continued to ache badly from the pain of separation from Robert. When you are separated from a soul mate, you miss your partner every minute of the day and most days are nothing more than a torture of aching and needing.

The soul mate connection is unlike a conventional relationship for, in these cases, the pain of separation doesn't lessen. Some days it feels as if your heart will burst out of your chest and fly to your true partner.

Fiona experienced all of this and more, although with readings and healing I was able to reduce the worst of the excesses and keep up her hope that the situation would resolve itself and

Robert would come back. At times, she would call in total pain and disbelief and ask how anything could hurt so much and why couldn't she just get over him?

As always, I explained that a connection so strong was something we have little control over and, in time, he would return. While we wait, all we can do is stay strong and accept what has happened. Trying to understand why just adds to the torture.

In time, Robert did contact her. Fiona, however, found it very difficult to talk to him. He frequently contradicted himself and didn't seem to have a clue what he was doing, how he felt or what he wanted. This, of course, made it much harder for her to be in contact with the man she loved so much, as she still struggled to make sense of why he had run in the first place.

This is a very common albeit totally bizarre and bewildering phase that nearly always occurs in these relationships. While the more aware soul feels the immense sense of pain and loss, the 'runner,' who mostly has a ton of issues, is absolutely confused by the power of the connection and will seem to contradict themselves and not know quite what's going on. It's common to hear 'I love you,' then a week later, 'I don't love you,' and a host of other seemingly weird behaviors.

Understand, however, that this is your soul partner struggling to understand what's going on within them, as they are also totally overwhelmed by the feelings and confusion that the connection brings.

At this point, I asked Fiona to trust me and to follow some simple rules for communication. She agreed when she realized the present interaction was confusing her even more. I asked Fiona to set out what she wanted from Robert, make it clear to him, then to back away. To insist that, if and when he called, she didn't want to hear how bad his life was, especially after she had offered everything to make him happy. And that if he could not be there for her, then to put the phone down.

Staying strong in this phase takes an awful lot of guts and faith when your runner seems so close to returning. To push them away unless certain criteria are met is scary when you so fear losing them again. But Fiona did it…

And, as in most cases, after a while it worked. It's said that runners return properly when the pain of separation is greater than the fear of commitment. And by refusing to negotiate on anything other than coming together properly, Fiona made Robert realize he had to face this once and for all or lose her.

They met, they talked, she called me. Robert had accepted he couldn't go on as he had and he was prepared to face his fears and give it a go. Many more meetings occurred before Fiona was sure he was ready and knew that he would face his fear of commitment.

When finally they both came together again, and had put the past behind them, Fiona asked Robert to come to me for a reading and consultation.

Seeing a runner face to face is a rare opportunity for me, because when most reconciliations occur, my work is done.

Robert arrived and it was apparent he had no idea what to expect. I gave him a psychic reading and saw what was going on within him and how he had struggled to make sense of the past couple of years. What he said was a real eye opener for me, a rare chance to see how the incredible intensity of a soul connection can scare the daylights out of someone seemingly so strong and together.

He started talking about a time before Christmas when he realized just how deeply he felt for Fiona and, although he had always shunned commitment of any sort, he had decided to ask her to marry him. On his way to buy a ring, he talked to a friend about marriage and said he suddenly became very scared and unsure. He never did tell me what the friend said but whatever it was plugged deep into his fears. After that, instead of asking her to marry him, Robert told Fiona it was over and that he had found someone else.

If you're astounded reading this, so was I when I heard it. His thinking was that he couldn't go through with it and maybe he wasn't good enough for her. What if he wasn't ready, what if it didn't work? All the other fear and insecurity-based questions rose up in him. His thinking was if she thought he had someone else, she could move on and not follow him. When runners run, they really do run. Robert had demonstrated absolute mastery of the runner 180-degree speed turn.

It was obvious that this man was unsure about himself—never mind what he could offer in a relationship. He made all his decisions from the head, not the heart. He mistakenly assumed Fiona could 'get over it.' It's one of the most frustrating things when runners make assumptions and don't give the other partner a chance. That's just what this one did.

However, now Robert was back and he was talking to me and that meant he wanted to understand what this was about and how he could deal with it. This was a terrific omen for the couple's future.

The outcome was that Robert did start to deal with his demons. His karmic lesson, his life transformation, the reason for this link, was to come to realize that he couldn't live life by purely mental decisions and fear. He learnt that his heart couldn't stay away and that fighting the connection only hurt them both and, ultimately, didn't work.

Fiona and Robert's married in Europe in July. Both transformed from their experiences of profound love and pain, their fears and worries are now a thing of the past, and both individually and together they are stronger, wiser and much more spiritually aware than before.

Destiny had her way.

I keep their wedding invitation, and many others, as a constant reminder that of all the hundreds of such cases I deal with most resolve happily.

I'm frequently told by 'authorities' on the subject that "soul mates rarely come together" and "only in the next life" and other such sayings...Well dear reader, have faith, because in my experience in the largest majority of cases that's not true...

That's why I'm writing this book

Chapter 2

How to Recognize a Soul Mate

There are no mistakes in God's world. Karma must be played out. We are here to support each other; we are all in the same boat—unknown

Soul mate is a term used commonly to describe our ideal partner for life, the person who's going to take our breath away, the person who's our perfect match in every way, who will understand us like no other and will finally make us feel totally happy and fulfilled—our 'other half.'

Search the Internet for 'soul mate' and you will find hundreds of results, most of which claim to be able to find your soul mate for you—guaranteed! Often couples refer to themselves as soul mates, the term seeming to proffer the fact that their bonding is unique and total and that they have found 'the one.'

Ok, so how do we know?

1. When we meet out soul mate?

2. We haven't met him/her already?

3. How to set out finding ours, if indeed we have one?

Firstly, let's clarify what we mean by a soul mate. In fact, there isn't just one type, there are several and not all of them are romantic or partnership situations. But for now, let's consider any type of special or unique connection with someone as a soul mate connection.

Anyone who has come into our lives and had a profound effect is, in some ways, a soul mate. They may have shared part of our life and taught us important lessons about our direction and ourselves. They have enriched and/or affected our lives in a deep and unusual way. We have a deeper connection with them than with others and know they will somehow change us.

Soul mates will vary in role, intensity, duration and outcome. Roles are teacher, student, healer and guide. In some cases, our soul mate will be a partner who makes us feel better than we have ever felt before and will restore our feelings of self-worth. Or it can be someone who hurts us but from whom we take forward a valuable lesson.

People in relationships often say things such as 'I thought s/he was my soul mate but it didn't last.' In these situations, their interpretation of soul mate means 'the one'—the connection for life. But as already mentioned, not all soul mate situations are purely romantic pairings and not all are meant to last a lifetime.

That person we thought was a soul mate and for life was certainly a soul mate on some level, but after they had fulfilled their destined time with us, it was necessary to part and move on. In other words, the connection was to enrich our lives but we were not destined to last forever as a couple.

But fear not, dear reader!!!!

We do have an ultimate 'one' who we may or may not find in this lifetime. But if we have met and lost a soul mate partner, we are already on the road to happiness, hard as that may seem to understand much of the time. For there are several soul mate connections on our way to ultimate happiness. Some will come and go and some will come and go and then return. And, ultimately, *one will stay.*

Right now, if you are missing someone so badly and can't possibly imagine that there could be anyone else, that concept will seem inconceivable. Trust me, I know, I've been there! In the beginning of a separation from your soul mate, the possibility that s/he won't return is a concept that simply can't be contemplated.

But trust that this amazing journey you are on is meant to lead you to your ultimate destiny and happiness. Destiny didn't do this by accident or just to hurt you.

To understand this, we need to look at the universe's reason for bringing soul mates of whatever sort to us and to realise what we are meant to gain from meeting them.

In each case where we meet someone special, someone unique with whom we share a special connection, s/he have been brought into our lives to share part, if not all, of our path and to bring us something valuable to take along on our journey.

For example, a soul mate can be a friend with whom we share a unique understanding, someone who knows us intuitively and with whom we have an instinctual pairing. They somehow know exactly who we are and how we work—in other words, they 'get' us. In this case, the person is someone we trust and depend on, someone who will act as a mirror to us, allow us to open up to our deepest emotions. With this soul mate, we share things we might normally not share with someone with whom we have a more conventional connection.

Or, a parent and one particular child can be soul mates. Although there is little to compare to the depth of a parent-child bond, sometimes the bond between one parent and one sibling can be especially unique and deep.

In all these cases, a profound and loving bond exists between these two people, working on a special level much deeper than others. The person brings something very special into our lives and, in many cases, the connection is positive and the bond will last even if the two people don't stay in touch.

Regardless, we learn something about ourselves and something about life from knowing this person, i.e. their soul and ours have paired for part of our spiritual journey throughout life. We have both been teachers and students. We have taught them something and they us. And, together, we have had experiences that we may not have had if we had not met.

In the case of an important lost love, s/he will have been a soul mate who came into our lives to share part of the path and to teach us something about love and about life, even though the parting may have been traumatic and painful. For whatever reason, the relationship had to end. We may not like this or agree that it had to happen, but it was an essential part of our spiritual and emotional growth to have experienced love and loss alike at that time.

So the reason for any soul mate is to share part of life's journey, its challenges and riches alike, to learn about ourselves and other people and to learn about life.

Many romantic soul mate pairs meet when at least one of the partners is already within a committed relationship, although I've yet to find one that was a fulfilling relationship. Most of these existing situations turn out to be in some way co-dependant and are based upon some practical consideration over and above the emotional, i.e. someone is 'secure' or trapped, depending on which way you look at it.

I'm sure that the timing of the soul mate meeting is no accident in these instances, as staying in situations that prevent us from living our lives to the full would not be 'allowed' by the universe. Thus we are pulled onto the new path by the soul connection—however hard it is to make the changes and however long it takes.

But what if we meet and connect with a soul mate but for some reason don't want to recognise the link or enter a relationship? Or we want the relationship, but our soul partner doesn't?

This is extremely common, as many of us act on what we think we *should* do and a timing that suits us rather than taking chances that come along when they come along. It's very common to hear people say they 'don't want a relationship right now' or are 'committed already' or 'aren't ready' for something so serious and intense or 'can't settle down yet,' for whatever reason.

Well. Here lies the first and probably the most important lesson in soul connections. And that is that these connections are made and managed by Madam Destiny in her infinite wisdom and, despite what we may 'want' or 'think,' she has many tools at her disposal to make sure we ultimately follow her path to unite with our romantic soul mate and to fulfil our time together, however long that may be.

The depth of soul mate connection varies depending on where we are on our soul path throughout our spiritual life. But a strong connection is, at the same time, amazing, incredible, profound and life changing. Add to that the almost unimaginable roller coaster of emotions and we know this isn't something we've imagined or manufactured or dreamed; nor is it something that anyone has allowed us to believe or manipulated us into.

But, despite these effects, we do often doubt and fear that somehow the connection is only one way or that we love them more than they love us or that this is unrequited love because, surely, if they felt like we did, they would run to us this very minute and put us out of our misery.

Fear not. If you have all the symptoms we've mentioned and your heart is screaming out that this person is the one for you like it never has before, then chances are you've got yourself a soul mate connection.

BUT there a process to go through until you can unite with your partner. It's complex and doesn't make much sense on a conventional level, but it has to happen this way because destiny is at work here.

How to Recognize a Soul Mate

- You met in unusual circumstances
- Feels like you've known them forever
- S/he isn't my normal type but there's just something about them.
- You don't need to speak to communicate
- Looking into their eyes, you see deep into their soul
- Your soul mate is on your mind 24/7 and you can't change that
- You sense your soul mate and know what they're thinking and feeling.
- Your interests change to more spiritual things
- Desperate to be with them and contact them all the time
- Feel totally at peace when you are with them
- Feel like a teenager again
- You know somehow you have changed and there's no going back

In many soul mate cases, one or both of the partners will be:

- Already in a relationship with some level of commitment but not emotionally satisfying
- Be scared of commitment
- Have been badly hurt in the past
- Suffered emotional problems
- Is still or has recently been in a controlling relationship
- Have moved from relationship to relationship, moving on when they are required to commit
- Most always, one of the partners will be sufficiently spiritually developed to understand the significance of this

relationship and that it is a life-changing event. And almost always one of the partners will be 'sensible' and try to 'do the right thing' on a very practical level.

Physical symptoms of soul mate connection:

- You feel like a different person, more alive

- A tugging feeling in the heart

- Headache behind the eyes

- Stomach churns and flutters

- Sleep patterns and diet will change

- Feeling 'lovesick'

- Sometimes, when you're apart, you feel a panic like you have lost someone close

- An overwhelming feeling that life is not worth living without the soul mate or, conversely, a new awareness that life must be worth holding on to if such feelings of love are possible.

Chapter 3

The One

I love, I have loved, I will love...I Capture the Castle by Dodie Smith

But back to the Internet dating agency that guarantees to find us 'the one,' the lifetime partner, the yin to our yang, the other part of us, our romantic life partner.

Firstly, nobody can find us our soul mate. As already discussed, soul mates are destined to come into our lives where and when they are meant to—at just the right time for us to continue on our journey of ever deepening spiritual understanding and emotional growth.

As we travel on our journey through life, we are not meant just to exist, to live, work, have children and then expire. Each of us has a spiritual journey, a journey of discovery of love and pain, gain and loss, adoration and hate, fear and hope, as we progress along our life path.

The universe doesn't really care if your car has a turbo or if the mortgage is paid off; she's most interested in the journey of the soul, in emotional and spiritual fulfilment, in the finding of 'ourselves.' She wants us to create only positive karma. That is why we must look deep inside and understand ourselves, shun negativity and hate and fear, learn to be strong and at the same time compassionate, learn to accept and to love and have faith and to do only good.

In other words, to accept and not need, to understand and not criticize, and to follow where our heart leads.

For each of us, this journey is a deep internal solitary one. Although we have friends and family, our soul journey of inner hopes and fears, dreams and disappointments, we will always seek that unique person who will connect with us on such a deep level that we will never feel alone.

And in fact 'the one,' the soul 'twin' is that person.

Soul Twins

Meeting the soul twin, sometimes referred to as twin flame, is quite a rare experience.

As we are all on a different part of our path and have different abilities to feel and understand love, how can we possibly know that our current relationship is as good as it gets? Soul mate relationships teach us, harden us, open us and help us grow spiritually until, if we are very lucky, we will be ready for the ultimate, the twin soul relationship.

At the time, we may not know if a relationship is transient or forever, but the dynamics are the same. And when we do reunite with a soul mate to work out the karma, who knows if it is for a day or for a lifetime?

But before we can ever get to the level where we have a possibility of 'forever,' we will have been through other soul mate relationships and have learnt some hard lessons, i.e. we will have loved and lost. This is the initiation of the person who is ready to meet the soul twin, the one eternal soul mate.

On the way to that ultimate pairing, our relationships and connections will have seen levels of love and pain that will have increased in intensity and thus the learning experience has become progressively harder.

However hard these experiences, though, we will have got over them in time. Although we may have some residual pain and regret, we will be able to move on to progressively deeper connections in due time.

The only connection that time never dulls and we never quite get over is the soul twin.

This process is illustrated by a story from the Middle Ages; a story that talks of an old and battered chalice. Chalices (or cups or goblets) were often used to symbolize the heart and its ability to carry emotion (as symbolized in the tarot suit of cups.)

Whilst new and shiny chalices were favored for drinking wine, the best and most sought after chalice was an old and battered one. This is because it had been tempered through time. It had taken knocks and scratches over the years and thus the metal has become progressively tempered and more resilient. The cup part of the chalice had gradually widened to hold more and more and the surety of its strength made it the best.

The tale parallels our heart's journey towards true soul twin love which requires that our connections increase in intensity and our hearts learn and temper through experience.

The symbolism here is of the heart needing to hold both love and pain on progressively more extreme levels before it is strong enough to hold the deepest and strongest love, that of a twin soul.

So how do we know where we are on the journey, how do we know, "Is this one the one?"

The answer is that we will not know, even as each progressive connection grows stronger and stronger. The main and undeniable difference between a soul mate and a twin soul is that once we have met a twin soul, being apart is the most difficult and painful experience of our lives and we just don't get over it.

Hard as that seems, the universe balances love and pain equally. As in the case of the chalice, we learn and develop and grow through a balance of both.

While counseling those in soul mate situations, I have heard many stories of love and loss. The next one I want to share is Susanne's. The beginning of her story shows how unusual circumstances led to her meeting Colin. This time, I'll let her tell you in her own words.

Chapter 4

Susanne's Story

"She gave you love and affection; Enough to weather any season; You found an excuse to walk away; But you didn't find no reason.." From *"How Bad Do You Want It?"—Don Henley."*

He had me with the can of tuna.

A statement that obviously requires a little explanation…

I don't actually remember meeting him. Looking back, it's as if one minute he wasn't there and the next he was and that was that. There's no memory of the first time I saw his face or the first words we spoke to each other.

I've experienced several periods in my life when the universe had her hand on my forehead, holding me back, forcing me to wait for a divine timing my impatience could only jeopardize.

My move to Los Angeles from Austin was the first time I ever felt the opposite…the universe pushing me forward in a way I had never experienced. Months before, I had closed my law practice, sold my house, moved to Austin to pursue my screen writing dreams. Austin, not LA, because my law license was only good in Texas and I wanted a fallback position.

The universe, however, didn't care—I was supposed to be in Los Angeles. When this became painfully obvious, it didn't matter that I only had three months left on my apartment lease.

Common sense would have said, hey! why move to LA on October 18 when you just have to come back to Texas for Thanksgiving and Christmas? Wait until that last day of December, finish up your lease, move out in the New Year.

If I had done that, I would never have met him.

So, the dog and cat and I packed it all up again and called U-Haul.

Not long after my arrival, I signed up for a UCLA night course on STORY ANALYSIS,, i.e. how production companies evaluate screenplays and determine if a script should become a film.

I read an article later that said pursuing a passionate interest often leads to the discovery of a soul mate. But I had abandoned any ideas of ever finding a perfect mate—all the energy and passion I might have had for a man now went into my writing. I had given up the search.

The class started in early January. When the professor walked in the door at the back of the room and passed by me (in my traditional back row seat), I was immediately besotted. He reminded me of an old boyfriend, whom I adored, and he was a charming and erudite performer who obviously fed off the energy in the room.

Most of the people in the class, however, had put in long days at the office and many had significant commutes. Nicholas's attempts to elicit a response, any response, from the class failed miserably. I tend to be low-key in group situations, which friends find hard to believe. I didn't want to be the one to speak up. But no one else was.

So I started answering his questions, hoping it would get the ball rolling. It did, but only between the two of us. The class quickly became a dialogue, until Peter finally said, 'Okay, WHO are you?" At least our comedy routine was waking everyone else up. (And only escalated as the semester went on, culminating in the night he called me a smart-ass and threw an eraser at me.)

When the three-hour class was over, Nicholas announced we were all invited to join him at a Japanese tearoom. I was familiar with the tradition of going out for a drink with the prof after class, but this was LA. Okay, I could roll with it. Green tea. Why not?

At this point, as everyone gathered up their belongings, people began to gravitate toward me. A girl on my right asked if I was going. I told her I was new in town and didn't know where the tearoom was and did anyone have a clue, because I was tired of getting lost in LA and driving around for hours.

Suddenly, a man in front of me answered the question for her. I hadn't noticed him during the class or at the break (and trust me, I might not be looking, but I had assessed the potential of every other man in the room). He had been in the first row, directly in front of me, out of my line of vision. He was perfectly pleasant-looking (in a bookish Harry Potter/Peter Parker way) and yes, he did know how to get to the tearoom.

His accent was English.

So the three of us ended up in my car, driving to Nicholas's after-class hangout. Where my dialogue with Nicholas continued while Heather and Colin (we being the only three to take up the offer) listened. I remember that I did ask Colin where he was from and he said England and I said of course but where, explaining I'd lived there junior year in college. (I found out later he had lived in America for a year in college.)

And I do remember driving us back to the parking garage and taking a closer look at him as we said goodnight. I thought he was five or six years younger than he turned out to be, so I remember wistfully thinking he was too young for me, even though he seemed like someone I would slot into the "possibility" category, i.e. there doesn't appear to be anything seriously wrong with him so he might be worth getting to know better.

No lightning bolt. No immediate flash of recognition.

I don't think he even crossed my mind in the next week or so, although I was looking forward to matching wits with Nicholas again. On the following Thursday, I went to the food court to get coffee before class. Colin was there and immediately sought me out.

That's the night my real memories of him begin.

He said he was surprised to see me because I had mentioned a conflict the week before. I had to think back...my new life was so full and so happy since I'd moved to LA—I was waking up to a new world and new people and new experiences everyday and couldn't remember ever being happier.

It took me a moment to recall that I had even had a conflict. I was touched that Colin remembered, gratified by his attention. Which, from that moment on, was unflagging. We talked before class, we talked at break, we talked after class at the tearoom.

We picked up two more regulars that second week—Keith, from New Zealand, and Joe, who lived on his boat an hour north of LA. Heather dropped out and though others would occasionally drop-in, our little group solidified.

Thursday became my favorite night of the week.

Colin and I slowly got to know each other better but he was still really not on my radar. As Joe said later, we always had our heads together, mainly because we shared an mutual passion for film—he saw an average of four films a week, which topped my two or three. He saw everything and I came to rely on him as my own personal movie critic, although we often had different responses.

I was planning a party so I could share all the diverse people I'd met with each other. One night, we discovered Nicholas was great friends with the Coen brothers and was actually one of the inspirations for a character in THE BIG LEBOWSKI. He went up several notches in Colin's book, where his stock was already pretty high, for the film was a favorite. I hadn't seen it, so I suggested we screen it at my house and why not do it the night of my party?

There was a screening room in my building with a small auditorium (I love LA!) So I gathered up email addresses so I could send out invites.

The night I had selected for the party happened to be Valentine's Day. I figured, why not? People can stop by the party for a while and if they have a significant other, they can then go out somewhere romantic. If they didn't, at least they weren't sitting home alone!

The Thursday night before the party, I grabbed a scoop of tuna salad from the food court to tide me over during class break. Colin approached, bearing a plate of French fries and onion rings.

"Tuna? Why tuna?" he asked.

I gave him the glossed-over version of "I had most of my pancreas removed after a car wreck and carbs are essentially off limits" and turned it around on him. He looked sheepish.

I don't eat meat," he said.

"Why not?" I asked, wondering about the sheepishness.

"I stopped a few years ago, when I was trying to balance my chakras."

He looked as if he expected me to tease him, but I casually responded,

"Oh, I have a video tape for that," and went on to the next topic.

He seemed pleased and relaxed back into our usual comfortable rapport.

After class, when we were all walking to the parking garage, I tried to get a count on who was coming to the party. Colin waffled a little, saying he liked to drink on Friday nights.

"Colin! You have to come, you have to come," I said. "You can drink at the party."

He didn't look convinced. I was surprised how disappointed I was.

So, on Valentine's Day night, as my guests spilled over into the atrium, I was taken aback as I rushed out the front door of my apartment. He was suddenly in front of me. We almost collided.

"Colin," I said, "You came!"

He was carrying two six-packs of Beck's and holding a small brown bag, which he held out to me. I'm sure my face reflected my surprise. I know, after I opened it, I was awash with emotions: pleasure, laughter, confusion, wonderment.

It was a can of gourmet albacore tuna. I priced it later at the health food store: $7!

I could only look at him.

"Happy Valentine's Day," he said. "I knew you couldn't have chocolate."

"Ohmigod," I answered. "Thank you."

That's when the lightning bolt hit.

We just stood in the doorway looking at each other. From his expression, I was inclined to believe he felt it too. Or maybe he was just feeling the singe that was coming from me and wondering why I was experiencing such a powerful reaction.

I mean, after all, it was only a can of tuna.

Wasn't it?

Nothing much changed after that, though, even though Keith asked me at the party how long Colin and I had known each other. I was taken aback, then remembered he hadn't been at the tearoom the first night. When I told him we had started talking that first night, Keith was surprised.

"You seem as if you've known each other forever," he said. "I thought you'd met long before the class."

We started emailing a little, but the tone was friendly, not flirtatious. He was a dependable, witty correspondent, though, and my heart sang when I saw his mails in my inbox.

My sister and her daughter were flying in from Texas and I mentioned we were going to Vegas and he gave me some money to put down on the roulette table. I lost it, but he forgave me. Part of me knew the crush was mutual; part of me wondered what the hell was taking him so long.

The last class of the ten weeks was rapidly approaching…surely, he would make some kind of move. Ask me to go to a movie with him, for God's sake. Or meet him for coffee on the weekend. Something that stopped short of an actual date but indicated a desire to deepen our connection. I was breathless with anticipation but nothing was happening.

The last night of class was the first night of the Gulf War. Nicholas was a Vietnam vet; I'd been late to class because of the peace demonstrations; helicopters were hovering everywhere over the UCLA campus; word came down that some British soldiers had already been killed.

The tearoom was somber. Nicholas said goodbye for the last time. Colin, Joe, Keith and I sat there after he left, cut loose, feeling adrift.

"We need to keep getting together," Colin said.

Finally!!

We all agreed.

"Well, we all know we have Thursday nights available. Let's just keep getting together every Thursday, here at the tea room," he suggested.

I was relieved, although slightly irritated that he'd managed to keep the connection going in a way that was not getting me any closer to a goodnight kiss!

But I thought about it long and hard. I was becoming attached. I didn't want to be attached. I didn't want to want him. So I decided it was just as well that he wasn't doing anything. Synchronicity wasn't finished yet, though, and the decision pretty much was out of my hands, even though I didn't know it yet. Two strange things happened in fast order.

One night, after an extremely irritating rejection received on a one-hour TV pilot I'd written, I couldn't seem to shake it off. Late that night, I decided I needed some serious distraction. So I signed up for match.com. Dating was looking like a breeze compared to this screen writing stuff. And, hell, Colin wasn't exactly beating down my door.

I spent a couple of hours on-line, selected four or five guys to send a brief note (picking the kind who are usually attracted to me—the engineer/CPA type), asking something innocuous like, "How's match.com working out for you and any suggestions on how to get the most out of it?"

The first guy wrote back that night. He hadn't spent all that money and time to sign up to give advice to someone. Okay, so he's off the list...

The universe stepped in again...turned out the guy in the office cubicle next to Colin's had posted his profile on match.com about an hour before I came online. Because he had spent over three months writing his profile before the post, receiving my email the next morning elicited this conversation...

"Colin! A woman has responded to my profile on match.com!"

"Really? Great!"

"Yeah. She's an attorney and a writer. I wonder if she's a screenwriter."

"That's funny. I know a woman who's an attorney and a screenwriter."

"Really? This one's from Texas and just moved to LA…"

"My friend is an attorney who's from Texas and just moved to LA!"

"She says she lives in Santa Monica."

"Let me see that…" By now, Colin was in his cubicle, checking out the email from me…

So our first meeting post-class found me being the one who was a little sheepish. Damn, I'm busted, being my response. I didn't want Colin to think I wasn't interested in him but, after all, he wasn't exactly moving the relationship along.

Keith didn't show (and never did again), so it was Colin and Joe and me.

We spent the evening getting to know each other better, without the parental and dominating presence of Nicholas. As would become our pattern, Colin and I would face each other and, as we were tuned into the same unique frequency, leave Joe sitting there feeling a little left out but glad to be off the boat and among friends, if nothing else.

Neither had been married before. Both had lived with two different women. Colin and I were both the oldest of three children. Colin and I had both been known to frequent psychics (one of the few men I'd met who would even admit something like that).

We had both traveled extensively—he'd worked in Turkey, I'd been to Istanbul and Ephesus and he was surprisingly pleased to find an American with a world-view—I'd said I'd traveled and I actually had.

He took yoga twice a week; I'd gotten to the graduate level in yoga before I'd had a car wreck that stopped my practice—I'd wanted to get back to it ever since.

And he drove an old Alfa Romeo…I'd had a '53 MGTD and a '65 Mustang until the brakes on the latter failed and I hit a tree, at which point my father said he would personally kill me if he caught me in another old car.

And, as I came to know from what I pieced together during all the time we spent together, Colin was blessed with an enormous capacity to love and an intense desire to connect with the right woman. So, when I won free tickets to a film screening with the screenwriter in attendance the next week, I invited my new "friend", via email, to join me.

After two days of no response (which was unusual), I emailed a second time. Yes, he had written right back to say he was on call at work that night and couldn't go—sorry I didn't get it. Yet he didn't counter with an alternative.

We were back to square one.

He said the evening seemed like something I could invite a match.com candidate to. I sensed he was fishing for whether my interest in him was platonic or otherwise—how was he supposed to interpret my invite? Since he had turned me down, I responded by saying it wasn't that kind of evening and just seemed like something he might enjoy.

No one was playing their hand.

I had lots of male friends I spent time with. If we were just friends, why was he so reluctant to move out of the prescribed box of Thursday nights?

Could it be because he was interested and wanted to take it slow? If we were just friends, why couldn't he make that clear, draw the line in the sand and put me out of my misery? And then maybe we could enjoy each other's company without what was increasingly feeling like a dishonest hidden agenda on my part.

I could not remember ever having a relationship with a man where the lines weren't drawn fairly early on You were married, living with someone, dating someone, available but gay, available but you're not my type, etc., etc.

I couldn't see any lines. He wasn't drawing any. Neither was I. So, define this relationship...please!

Stalemate.

A week or so later, I emailed him that I might not make Thursday night because Wednesday was my birthday and I was going to take myself to Vegas to celebrate. He wrote back immediately that he had just celebrated his birthday the previous weekend by taking himself to Vegas!

I read later that soul mates are often born under the same sign. We were both Tauruses.

At this point, I did what most women would do. I called in a girlfriend.

By now, we had switched to Colin's hangout—a T.G.I.F.'s midway between my house and Joe's boat. My wonderful friend Sheila agreed to go with me, because she had recently had what she termed "transcendent truck sex" with a fellow surfer who was not pursuing her as ardently as their encounter might have warranted and she wanted male input—Colin and Joe were dying to hear the details!

Her conclusions?

"Well, I may be having transcendent truck sex but you and Colin have a real relationship and it's clear you both care a great deal about each other."

"Yes, but is he interested in me?"

She thought about it. "I don't know."

"Is he not interested in me?"

"No, I didn't pick up that, not at all."

"Well, is it glaringly obvious that I'm interested in him?"

"No, not at all. It's not obvious at all. He's a great guy, though.

Incredibly insightful and sensitive. But obviously wounded."

And so…what now?

The evening did clear up one thing up for me, though. When Colin breezed in that night, late, he had extended a handshake as a form of apology.

When he took my hand, and I felt the strength and warmth of his, I was a goner. The mental intimacy was suddenly deepened by a strong physical attraction, that magnet pull, for the first time.

Later that night, as I squeezed back into the group after returning from the "loo," my hands briefly brushed his back. My knees almost went weak. Despite the fact I hadn't wanted to get attached. Despite the fact that I had no idea what the hell was going on. It was too late to worry about it.

It was a done deal.

He wrote that he had enjoyed meeting Sheila. I wrote back that she had enjoyed the evening, too, but wouldn't be a regular participant. He wrote back that she must not have liked him.

I wrote back, "Nonsense. Sheila was amazed and amused by the hidden depths beneath your mild-mannered exterior."

He responded, "Mild-mannered? When are women going to realize that I'm sexy and dangerous?"
I wrote back, "Of course we realize that. We just don't want to let you know that we know."

The next week the universe stepped in again.

Joe, because he was JUST my friend, helped me move that Thursday, into what was hopefully a more economical apartment.

Colin, granted, lived on the other side of the hill and worked long hours, so he hadn't offered to help. But when we'd finished, Joe's cold had worsened so he went back to the boat. Colin had never given any of us his phone numbers so I had no way to get in touch with him, since my ISP wasn't up yet. So I braved the three freeways and the hour of traffic that it took to get to T.G.I.F.'s, intending to stay just a little while and then come home to unpack boxes.

I remember clearly thinking while I sat in the 405 gridlock—this is such a waste of time. He wasn't interested—get it through your thick skull. But maybe I could get a definitive answer once and for all. Even that would be a relief.

He was late, again, but we spent the next four hours talking nonstop.

For me, it was as if we were the only two people in the bar. We talked about everything, anything. I'm a communicator and I can often overwhelm the person I'm speaking to if they don't make the effort to stay up.

I have to remind myself to draw the other person out, because I don't need drawing out and I forget it's something other people might require. But this was so effortless...so easy...such an intimate connection with a man, unlike anything I had ever experienced. Like two pieces of a puzzle that fit snugly together.

I floated through the next week, although there was no change in the tone of his emails. Joe cancelled the next week, too, and Colin wrote and said I was off the hook if I wanted to be. I wrote back and said that I hadn't signed up for a new class because he and Joe were such cheap entertainment and I would still like to come.

When I showed up, some people from work were with Colin. He grabbed me as I walked by, nearly missing him since I wasn't used to him showing up on time.

As I squeezed into the barstool next to him, he didn't move turn away or move his body back to make it easy on me. I had to brush against him to climb up on the stool. Then, he patted me on the arm and said it wouldn't be long and his "work colleagues" would be gone and we'd have "just you and me time."

Finally. I felt as if we were together and it was all unspoken. It just was.

He was so relaxed, so in charge, so happy, despite a gout attack that had caused a week of frustration and emergency room visits for him. His bar buddies came and went but toward the end of the evening, one hung around—another Keith.

He wasn't a bad guy, but he and I had never connected. I felt left out, excluded. Colin didn't seem to notice.

The guy on my right did, though. He was in an expensive suit, expensive watch. Very attractive. After awhile, it became apparent to me he was trying to cut me out of the herd. I wasn't trying to make Colin jealous, but I was feeling a little ignored, so I was friendly when the man spoke to me.

I had turned to get the bartender's attention to settle my bill (although Colin usually insisted on treating me, I didn't want him to think it was expected.)

The handsome stranger and I exchanged a few more words. Colin didn't notice. He left for the bathroom. When he came back, it hit him. The guy was flirting with me.

Suddenly, it was clear Colin took the loss of my attentions as a personal rejection. The air went out of him. An actor friend explained it to me later—it's the alpha wolf syndrome. This other guy was obviously affluent, confident and he was not afraid to make a move. Colin compared himself and found himself lacking…I can't fight you for her, so take her. I didn't want the other guy. I wanted Colin.

From the open, warm posture he'd extended me all night, he closed up, his shoulders hunched, he almost seemed to shrink.

"Do you want me to leave?" he asked.

"Of course not. Don't be silly!"

I immediately turned my full attention back to him. But he was gone. I couldn't get him back. I thought he'd fight for me, let me know he didn't want me flirting with anyone else, that we were together. But he didn't. And no matter how I tried for the next twenty minutes or so, he wouldn't re-connect.

So I slid off the barstool.

"Next week?" he said, and his voice held a note of panic and lack of control I'd never seen.

He was actually showing an emotion. Looking back, I'm sure that momentary lapse was hard for him.

"Of course."

So I left. Thinking he'd tease me about the guy in his next email. Thinking he would tease me about it the next week. That's what he always did with Helen, his bar buddy. Like a mischievous little brother. But it was never mentioned between us again. It was as if the whole evening never happened.

Sheila, Joe, Colin, Keith the bar buddy and I got together the next week. Colin was jovial, but not once during the entire evening did we break off into smaller groups, as usually happened (i.e. Colin and I had no "just you and me" time).

He did, however, lead the group discussion and asked each of us in turn such questions as, "What are you looking for in a relationship?" and "Have you ever had phone sex?"

I just watched him, amused but not sure how to take it all. The questions were too hot topic to ask me when we were talking alone. He clearly wanted the answers, though.

"So, Susanne, what are you looking for?"

"A good heart," I answered immediately.

He was taken aback. "Surely, there's more than that?"

"No. That's it."

He seemed perplexed. So was I.

So that Saturday I sent him another email. I told him I'd had time to think about what I was looking for and discovered I did have a few things to add. I wanted someone with a wicked sense of humor, someone who loved movies and travel (including occasional trips to Vegas), someone who liked my dog (she had spent the whole party in his lap!) but the cat was optional.

On Monday, he wrote back that since Joe was going out of town for a month and he had decided to hit the gym every night in an effort to forestall another gout attack, Thursday nights were off for the time being and he hoped I didn't mind.

Mind? Mind? I was devastated.

I retreated to a place of rejection that felt very familiar, the place I was trying to avoid when I hadn't wanted to get attached at the beginning. How could I be so stupid?

But no matter how I tried to reconcile the rejection with the reality, it wouldn't mesh. He couldn't be rejecting me. It just didn't connect. It just didn't FEEL right. What the hell was going on?

That was the first time I talked to a psychic, a fellow screenwriter I'd met in an on-line class. No, Colin was not rejecting me. He was taking a break from everyone. He lacked the self-confidence to see that he could be a potential partner for me. He was afraid of getting hurt. He wanted to control his emotions. He would be back.

I wanted to believe her. I didn't think I could.

Steve's Analysis

Susanne's story follows a very familiar theme. The initial gentle but magnetic attraction, the getting to know each other followed by the WHAM, the point of connection. Others thinking the couple had known each other for a long time is also a key indicator of the obvious ease and 'rightness' of the energy between them. This point is often referred to as the 'recognition' meeting, as we recognise someone we have known from a past life (more about that in the next section).

As if to underline the cosmic forces behind this meeting, Madam Destiny, of course, showed her hand through the coincidences or synchronicity that occurred throughout the period: all seeming to point towards this being something very special.

It may seem bizarre that after Colin insisted on meeting regularly, he ran for the hills. However, it's not surprising, as he clearly saw the potential for this link and then realised after a short time that it was maybe much deeper than he could handle.

I believe the psychic friend got that right—this is someone who realised he needed to keep control of his emotions as he remembered a time when he was badly hurt. Meeting Susanne stirred up a whole nest of insecurities and inner demons from his past, so Colin became a classic soul mate runner.

Chapter 5

Karma — The Universal Law of Destiny and Balance

For every event that occurs, there will follow another event whose existence was caused by the first, and this second event will be pleasant or unpleasant according as its cause Pleasure and pain come from your own former actions (karma). Thus, it is easy to explain karma in one short sentence: If you act well, things will be good, and if you act badly, things will be bad.

H.H. *the 14th Dalai Lama*

Q. So why does all this happen and what's going on to make me feel like this?

If you talk to a psychic or someone familiar with soul connections, a most often mentioned subject is past-life connections.

It is generally accepted in metaphysics that we come into this life having agreed to connect with certain spirits, a decision we made when leaving the last life on this planet. At that time, for some reason, our business with them could not be completed and thus we meet again to continue our mutual destiny.

What gives this theory some weight when we meet our soul connection is the immediate recognition of 'Don't I know you?' and the feelings of familiarity and 'home.'

The truth of it is that our spiritual energy and the other person's are connected and thus we communicate with them and their feelings at a deep spiritual 'psychic' level.

Between the two, there's a knowing and understanding that doesn't need to be verbally communicated. When we see them, our hearts go mad and all our senses tell us this person is someone very special to us.

Friends may say it's sexual attraction or us looking for a 'type' or some other sort of reason for the attraction but deep within we know there's something a lot more—a reason for us to meet.

So the basis of soul mate connections on any level is to resolve karma. Much as we may not like or understand this and want to 'opt out' of having to go through the experience, karma has to be lived. There is no 'get-out-of-jail-free' card.

To understand karma, we have to at some level accept that we come back to have several lives and carry forward issues and connections from one incarnation to the next.

We often hear from psychics and counsellors on soul mate relationships that there is a karmic debt, i.e. some unfinished business between the two souls that requires that we reconnect with that soul in this lifetime to resolve the issues or 'karma.'

Think of karma as a sort of cosmic bank balance where credits and debits of our actions toward other people are required to be settled within a lifetime, i.e. our balance of good and bad deeds is zero or above. Also added to this account is "did we truly follow our hearts and our destiny?" or did we 'Know better?'

If not, then the concept we are talking about here is that unfinished business has to be completed and will follow us through many lifetimes, i.e. we must always follow our hearts even when it may be the hardest thing to do and we must always do good to others, whatever the circumstances and whatever they did to us.

Much is written about karma and past-life connections and, although I tend to agree with a lot of it, I find it can be very confusing for most people to consider all of the implications of unfinished business from a previous incarnation that ties them to a soul mate in this lifetime.

Likewise, I meet a lot of people who are told that they won't be with their soul mate in this life but that their connection will go through to their next life on this planet, when it will be resolved.

This academic metaphysical explanation is all very well but many, including myself, don't find it much practical use when we have live this life in the now with all its pain and challenges. On the question of karmic learning and being tested, to most of us the thought of another painful lesson is as useful as a chocolate teapot. How is more pain going to help us?

The key question is 'What more do we need to learn?' We each have to decide that for ourselves and, quite often, we won't realize until we have learnt the lesson. Through this pain, we often discover something about ourselves that had never really come to the fore previously.

In many cases, we lose interest in our jobs and things that once satisfied us and we set off in a new direction. The lesson therefore may very well be that we are forced to follow our hearts and can no longer stay in situations that don't fulfill us.

Security and fear and convention are often thrown out the window. And, then, just when we thought that was all, karma may have another lesson, no matter how much we don't want one. If it is Madam Destiny's decision, we get it, regardless.

Reassurance comes with the surety that what must be must be. If karma must be done, then we know this path is meant to lead somewhere good.

Simply speaking, karma is the universal law of destiny and balance, i.e. we all have a destined 'karmic' path and along that path we create karma, either good or bad. This is quite simple to understand in terms of modern sayings such as 'What goes around, comes around,' 'Do good, get good; do bad, get bad,' and what's commonly known as the rule of threes, 'Whatever you do, good or bad, comes back to you threefold.'

I don't think many people would have a problem accepting that concept of doing good and staying positive because it returns to us, although not necessarily in the ways we would like.

For example, if we help an old lady across the road, it's unlikely someone is going to come up and help us across the road, especially as we may not need that help. But according to the rules of karma, something nice, however small, will happen to us at a later time.

This is an example of our general karma where the person for whom we did the good deed won't necessarily repay us, but the universe will recognize our kindness and repay it in some other way. Perhaps, simply, the satisfaction of doing a good deed will be its own reward. Regardless, the rules of karma have been obeyed, i.e. a balance has been achieved.

Unlike our general karma, created by acts such as helping the old lady across the road, karma with our soul connection exists only between the two parties and can't be repaid by anyone or anything else, only by an act of our partner. This is because the karma between us was established in a past life and remains owing as we entered this world.

As mentioned before, karma is like a bank balance and we and our soul mate have between us some form of unsettled karmic debt. Therefore, we are brought together by destiny to settle this debt. As many psychics and spiritualists will tell you, if that karma isn't settled in this lifetime, then it goes on to another and another and another.

However, my belief is that destiny will do whatever she can to help us to be together with our soul mate and settle things in this lifetime. If someone tells you it will go forward, don't despair. It's never too late to be together in this life, whatever the circumstances. The universe has many powers at her control and she can change our lives in a day, so never give up hope and know that she's working for you!!

So when we get together, what is this debt and how do we settle it?

In most cases, the debt is some failure to be together as a pair to fulfil some pre-destined purpose. This may be for any amount of time and almost any purpose. To understand this, we have to accept that destiny has a reason for two people to be together and that events in the universe don't happen randomly—there are no coincidences!

Often, this connection happens to lead us on our correct life path. For reasons that we won't know, we are destined to be with this person. But with soul mates, it's never that easy. For most soul mates to come together, there are many hurdles to cross, i.e. the rules of karmic balance mean that nothing is for free!!

Usually, each soul mate will have to come to terms with much inner conflict and/or residual insecurity and, most of all, and in my case hardest of all, learn to be patient.

As discussed previously, we ascend different levels and learn different lessons as we progress along our life path. Often, when we meet our soul mate, one of us is with someone else or is afraid of the intensity of the connection and things are far from easy. So meeting them is just the start of an even more amazing journey that anything that has come before.

Chapter 6

Delia's Story

"All truth passes through three stages. First, it is ridiculed. Second, it is violently opposed. Third, it is accepted as being self-evident."
- Arthur Schopenhauer (1788-1860)

I am not 'with' Jim anymore.

From the day I met him, I knew this was the man I deserved to be with, the one who would never leave my soul. Yet I fought it too. I didn't want to feel that way about anyone. After a year of an on/off relationship, he told me that the happiest times he has had have been the times he spent with me, he told me that he trusts me more than he has ever trusted anyone, that he likes me enormously, that he enjoys my company so much, that we are such good friends, that he cares about me enormously, that he likes sleeping with me more than he has liked sleeping with any woman…but he sees no future for us.

I found that hard to understand. Of course, it's exactly the way I feel about him. He has just described to me the perfect relationship and I struggled to understand why he did not love me as I had come to love him. We were so incredibly good together.

My relationship with Jim came so naturally. As I said to him, "Yes, we have everything going for us…but it's not going anywhere." And his response: "No, I don't think it will." And I wanted to shout at him, "WHY NOT?"

"You need to meet someone who will be serious with you," he said to me.

"And sadly, it's not me," he added. "This isn't love for me, but I couldn't have come through these last months without you. You will always be my best friend, I love you as much as I have loved any woman, without actually being 'in love', and I want to keep you in my life as my friend, my confidante and my lover, but know I can't."

Confused? Me too!

All that is what he said to me over 10 months ago…and we are still caught in this loop. He still won't let me go, even as he tells me he is so in love with someone else.

Only a few days ago, he said, "Just because it hasn't ultimately worked out does not mean that between you and me I did not love you profoundly." But he never told me he loved me when we were together. When I asked him why not, what was the worst thing that could have happened, he said 'that you would end our relationship.'

I still can't understand it. There is no point in trying to understand. He is working on an entirely different level.

Every time we have contact, he tells me it is the very final, final time. Yet within days he is back, saying 'meet me,' even as he tells me he is deeply and seriously in love with someone else. During this time, he has been 'in love' with two other women, both of whom he has described as the 'love of his life.' "But actually,' he said the other day, "I will never reach a place where I don't need you and want you…"

Until he says something like that, I can convince myself that this is all in my head, that I have blown the whole thing up into something it isn't, because if you care that much for someone, why walk away from them? I don't ask for these comments, I never put him on the spot, I never contact him. He has no need to feed my ego or my vanity.

We've been apart for the best part of a year. Perhaps I survive by holding on to the belief that ultimately destiny will sort this out; I think I have been through with him the first two parts of the quote above…now I'm just waiting for the final stage…for him to accept his love for me as self evident…maybe he's getting there!

> *"Another love before my time, left you sad and blue;*
> *Now my heart is paying for things I didn't do;*
> *The more I try to show I care, the more we drift apart;*
> *Why can't I free your doubtful mind and melt your cold, cold heart ?"*
> —Hank Williams

Steve's Analysis

Delia's situation displays some of the 'classic' elements common to soul mate relationships. Whilst she can accept the connection, the power of the emotions and the 'pull' between them, Jim obviously can't deal with their intensity. Even though he's tried and tried to pull away, the fact that he can't is clear evidence of the connection and his need to keep her in his life.

When I read this man, it's apparent he has emotional issues and sees 'love' as something he decides rather than experiences, also evident to me through his past 'loves' who come and go with regularity.

I'm sure he sees the real love he has for Delia as a sort of dependence and is totally scared by the connection, not realizing that this is the real thing and this love will heal him rather than hurt him.

As in all soul mate connections, he will be forced to change and become aware that there is no way out of this until he faces his fears. The only variable is how much pain and emptiness he's prepared to live with and for how long.

Because be in no doubt—being apart from one's soul mate is a painful and empty existence.

Chapter 7

Free Will

"Human beings, vegetables, or cosmic dust, we all dance to a mysterious tune intoned in the distance by an invisible player". Albert Einstein

Q. My soul mate and I are apart because s/he wont accept what we have between us, so how does this make any sense if it's destined???

Many people will ask what is destined and what isn't. Often a psychic will say that one member of a soul pairing is exercising their 'free will' and choosing not to continue the connection.

Without doubt, we believe we have a very high degree of control over our lives because of our free will. Free will to choose our houses, colour of our car, hairstyle and many other things.

But does our free will extend to choosing our destiny or our ultimate life path? The answer is intimately no. As discussed, karma will push and push and push us in the direction she wants us to go and our part is to learn to lose our fear and go with it, to let it happen. Each time we refuse to do that, things get harder and harder...

So what about our free will: how does it affect our path?

If birth and death are destined, how come we as the human race can believe this free will allows us to choose ALL that happens in between?

The example of the mouse in the laboratory maze further explains my theory on free will and karma.

If the entry to the maze represents birth and the exit death, then the maze itself represents the paths and options mapped out for us, i.e. our karmic path. Within these options, we do have free will. For example, our little mouse friend comes to a crossroad on his journey through the maze.

Right is the exit but that corridor is a little dark and foreboding. So the mouse turns left.

He has to go through some cold water but he presses on.
At the next food point, there's no food.

The next stage, he is scratched and scraped by rough terrain.
Until finally he arrives at a crossroad.

The *same* crossroads.

This explains one reason psychics will tell you that they have trouble predicting time. Our free will is at work as we learn our lessons. We can follow the path, we can use our brains, we can

'Know better,' but we only delay the inevitable. We can't change *what* but we can change *when*!

After all, destiny did equip us with a map—it's called the heart. When we learn to follow it, we are on the path.

Jayne's story

I suppose from my own experience, I can say that the separation from him is terrible. I have extremely strong feelings for him and constantly worry.

Things seemed to be going fairly well for us, but we have not seen each other since February. It is like something is stopping us from meeting or communicating properly or progressing this relationship. We have had so many aborted meetings now. During this year, he has lost his job, has a mother with cancer, financial worries, a sick brother...the list goes on.

It doesn't help that we are both with other people, as the sense of guilt is overwhelming. But there is hope and we are hanging on to that.

Chapter 8

Synchronicity

"Nature does nothing uselessly"—Aristotle

Synchronicity is the universe's mechanism for what we often refer to as coincidence.

In and around soul mate connections, synchronicity usually shows itself in all sorts of weird coincidences and events—as if to confirm that destiny is at work here and we need to know it.

Examples of simple synchronicity are when times are hard financially and, just as you feel things are at their worst, something comes along. Or when you've been thinking of someone you haven't heard from for a long time and then they call out of the blue. Or when you have been thinking about this person and suddenly their favourite track comes on the radio.

Synchronicity is why no buses arrive, then three come at once. Like karma, it's another universal tune to which we dance. If karma is the lesson and the reason why we have to do things, synchronicity is the when.

Synchronistic events usually surround important life experiences and are especially prominent around soul mate relationships. I'm betting that when you met your soul mate, it was as if a handful of coincidences conspired to help you meet yet it felt like an accident.

Likewise, throughout the path of the relationship, whether together or apart, certain weird and bizarre coincidences will have occurred. For example, if your soul mate's name is Susan, you look up at the TV and the presenter's credit pops up as a Susan. Then, you open the newspaper and the first headline has the name Susan. Later, in the car, you turn on the radio and the first song, yup, you guessed it…is about someone called Susan.

My belief is that this mechanism serves as an indicator that destiny is behind the processes that steer us through this important and challenging part of our life. It's like a cosmic reassurance that someone actually is in the driving seat and so we can have confidence that the journey is not a random one.

Psychologist Carl Jung believed the traditional notions of causality were incapable of explaining some of the more improbable forms of coincidence. Jung believed that, when no causal connection can be demonstrated between two events, but where a meaningful relationship nevertheless exists between them, a wholly different type of principle is likely to be operating. Jung called this principle "synchronicity."

In *The Structure and Dynamics of the Psyche*, Jung describes how, during his research into the phenomenon of the collective unconscious, he began to observe coincidences that were connected in such a meaningful way that their occurrence seemed to defy the calculations of probability.

"A young woman I was treating had, at a critical moment, a dream in which she was given a golden scarab. While she was telling me this dream, I sat with my back to the closed window. Suddenly I heard a noise behind me, like a gentle tapping. I turned round and saw a flying insect knocking against the windowpane from outside. I opened the window and caught the creature in the air as it flew in.

It was the nearest analogy to the golden scarab that one finds in our latitudes, a scarabaeid beetle, the common rose-chafer (Cetoaia urata) which contrary to its usual habits had evidently felt an urge to get into a dark room at this particular moment. I must admit that nothing like it ever happened to me before or since, and that the dream of the patient has remained unique in my experience."

What's difficult to comprehend in synchronicity is cause and effect, as in Jung's example. Did the woman or the scarab cause the effect? Or, the more likely and my personal belief, the event was pre-destined and therefore inexplicably intertwined events had to happen together, or synchronistically.

I like to see these events as a reassurance from the cosmos that this part of our life path is subject to destiny's control and she's just reminding us that we're going to be ok…Important synchronistic events will surround an important time in our relationship. So, if suddenly you spot some of these seemingly bizarre coincidences, then be assured an important event isn't far away.

Chapter 9

Rick's Story

Rick's story illustrates how a very strong connection can change our life completely in a very short space of time.

I walked onto a film set and she seemed to appear from nowhere. I knew many of the crew, but this face was new. She introduced herself and I realized she had the most beautiful eyes I had ever seen.

As the days went by, I found myself going onto set again and again, always hoping to see her. As soon as she saw me, she came over and we talked and laughed nervously like a couple of school kids

That first weekend, she was on set and I was at home but I just couldn't get her out of my mind. Whatever it was I had seen in her eyes was haunting me and the weekend seemed to go on forever. My partner kept asking what was wrong with me and all I could say was that I didn't know. But what was 'wrong,' if it could be wrong, was that I just wanted to see her again.

What was happening to me??? I couldn't understand what mechanism had made me feel like this, but I had a feeling that meeting her had somehow changed my life, changed me, and there was no going back.

That Monday, we met on set and went for a walk in the lunch break. She admitted she had missed me all weekend and the next thing I knew, I kissed her. What made me do it, I don't know, but nothing ever felt so right.

Every day I saw her was living and loving on a level I had never even dreamed about. Life before had been in black and white compared to this new color 3D world we now both inhabited— basically, the world had suddenly become an amazing place. We were both wowed by being together and I knew in my heart that my lifelong search was finally over. I had found where I belonged; it wasn't a place, it was with this person. This was home.

We used to just sit and talk in the sunshine for an entire day without realizing the sun had gone down. Work and other practical matters faded into insignificance compared to what was happening between us. We missed each other every minute of every day and neither of us slept during this period.

Both of us had come to the conclusion that it was time to tell our live-in partners that it was time to separate, but not to mention a third party to avoid unnecessary pain. We both were in similar situations where the relationships had stayed together when they should have been terminated a long time before, but like a lot of people we hung on to avoid hurting anyone and because I guess we got used to it.

We each went through that painful process and stayed strong through our love for each other and our plans for the future. She took me to meet her parents and I felt like a million dollars as we talked about our future. The parents gave me the impression that they were relieved to see their daughter so happy. Although HE wasn't talked about, I knew I was accepted. Back at home, it was a difficult time, but we both got through it in our own way and arranged to meet her parents for a second time to have dinner and tell them more about our plans.

The night before we were due to meet her parents for the second time, I returned home where I knew things would be bad because of the separation and living in separate rooms while the practical things were worked out. But, on arriving, I was greeted by my ex-partner, very drunk, who told me that she had an anonymous call from a man telling her everything.

I couldn't believe it, the detail was incredible, and it was totally damning, making it seem as if I was someone who cheated on a regular basis and this was just another conquest. It was designed to do the maximum damage and it did.

I called Suzie and told her what had happened and she said "Oh my god, I have to tell him now" and cried. What happened after that is like a bad dream. A month or two later, I found myself living in a rented house completely on my own and Suzie had told me she didn't want a relationship with me and didn't love me. I had a hole in my heart the size of a planet and I wanted to curl up and die. I lost lots of weight and was told I looked like a heroin addict.

The following few months were a pit of despair and pain like I never knew existed. Suzie and I did meet again at a Christmas party and the inevitable happened. She kissed me and cried her eyes out and told me she was so deeply in love with me. Then, two weeks later, after little contact, she announced she was happy and staying with him.

How can you describe those times when life is so bleak and you hurt so much that every day is a month of pain and sometimes you pray to die? Pain doesn't describe it. I had lost enormous amounts of weight and used to physically throw up every night thinking of her with him.

I wasn't just looking into the abyss. I was in it.

My ex-partner went for the jugular and took as much money from me as she could in the separation. I was in no state to fight. But that wasn't a problem because I had a good job.

Well, I did, until a month later.

I had been very successful in a short period time and, like it or not, that made me a target for some of the more established executives in the business. Most were happy to share in the mutual success, for this was a point I always made—that we were a team and the team worked as one entity. But, for one or two, this painted a huge target on me as they saw my success as somehow embarrassing for them.

After I had returned from time off to deal with the worst of the angst and grieving, I was called in to the office. They had done their work well...

All the success was suddenly attributed to accident and fate and 'would have happened anyway' and anything less than perfect was personally my fault. Even the most successful business decisions were deemed to have been made by random actions and actually only 'seemed' successful. The once widely applauded entrepreneurial spirit had suddenly become a refusal to toe the line and was a 'problem.'

The ludicrous 'facts' being presented to me were laughable and when I pointed out the glaring contradictions in what was being presented, I was accused of being defensive.

What had been conveniently forgotten was that just a month before I had been paid a record bonus (I expect it was a larger one than my boss!) and received a letter congratulating me on the success of the businesses I had built, which had returned such good results that I was receiving this five figure cherub.

It was very clear that the people who had seen me as a threat now realized I was on the back foot in my personal life and they used that time to pull the trigger...

I walked from the office and got into my car.

This whole situation was so ludicrous and contrived that anyone could see through it. I called my lawyer and he said it was a simple case. After a long and drawn out legal interchange, the tables had turned and I had proven the many contradictions and falsities in their story, making it glaringly obvious to anyone that it was contrived and, if turned sideways, wouldn't even cast a shadow. Even to the point that their chief executive changed his statement five times and his lawyer, utterly frustrated, admitted to me in a moment of candor that their case wouldn't hold water and I had them over a barrel.

Naively, I had assumed that things would be redressed and that some sizeable settlement or offer of a meeting would be forthcoming. But, no, they stuck it out. So I received my contractual figure and walked away. A tribunal would have torn a hole the size of a mountain in the company's case but I didn't have the strength to fight because of what I was going through personally—and they knew it.

Those months felt like I had ceased to exist. You may be thinking, pull yourself together and get over it. Most of my friends did and, as the months went by, they understandably became increasingly bored with hearing about it and subsequently concerned that I was losing touch with reality. For some reason, they didn't seem to realize how startlingly obvious their comments where. Excuse me, do you think I haven't tried!

I reasoned that this was just a painful separation and bad luck and that I would get over it…but I wasn't getting over it. Love and pain are no strangers to me—I had loved and lost enough times to know that it damn well hurts and, however much it hurts, you heal and get over it.

My wife had left me a year after we were married and I had hurt, hurt like hell. The pain and confusion had been extreme and it had taken a huge amount out of me. But, after a year, I had healed and was getting over it.

If it was like that with a woman I had married, how could I possibly be going through a hundred times worse with someone I hadn't even had a long term relationship with?? It made no sense. Added to that, my career was on the floor, both of these, as I could see it, through no fault of mine.

A close friend looked into my eyes and said I just wasn't there. True, it felt like my spirit had left my body. Some times I didn't even feel like I existed.—the loss was on a level so deep I had lost myself. I didn't know who I was or what the hell was happening.

I hadn't had a great life and had experienced a lot of pain and disappointment; apparently, more than most. But each time, however hurt, I had got up and somehow started again. Whether personal or professional, I had overcome the trial and fought on. Now I'd met the love of my life and she had been snatched away and, shortly afterwards, my job too.

I hated the universe. For God's sake, stop shooting the phoenix!!

She did contact me from time to time, wanting to be friends. I tried, but how could I? How could this woman who said she loved me more than she could imagine just change her mind like that and suddenly want to be friends? Couldn't she understand how I was hurting and how I could just not understand what had happened? I hadn't changed and I didn't do anything to affect the situation; someone else did.

To add a further level of insanity, she told me she didn't want me to be with anyone else because it would hurt her. She begged me to stay in her life…

This wasn't just absurd, it was obscene and surely it was some practical joke.

I'm very aware that if I was reading this, I would say, "Hey, guy, you've been played," or I would observe that she was in a terrible relationship and needed an escape and it just got out of hand but she was never going to leave him. And all of these would be reasonable assumption, given the facts.

A lot of people offered that to me and said she didn't want to hurt you and that maybe she was scared and a host of other perfectly logical explanations.

But I had seen something they hadn't and felt something they hadn't. I had seen the love in her eyes, the tears of pure and overwhelming emotion at being together. I had felt her heart and experienced the utter and indescribable magic of being together.

More than that—even after a year and a half of not seeing her or hearing from her, my being is as tied to hers as the day we first connected. You don't get over it, you just live with it.

What we have is way way beyond any sort of love on a conventional level. We are meant to be together. I accept that she has decided, for whatever reason, that she doesn't want that. But our connection, our tie, is at a level that ignores what either of us want. I feel her and I know she feels me.

What will happen is in the hands of destiny and I now accept that.

Steve's Analysis

In Rick's case, he clearly had to undergo tremendous change all at once. We have to ask the question, if he hadn't met Suzie, would he have stayed in a relationship and job that weren't right for him and was this the only way to make him change path?

Suzie was clearly scared of the connection and wasn't able to cope, especially since someone had intervened and stirred things up by informing Rick's girlfriend, most probably to make him withdraw from Suzie.

Suzie's relationship is very much a 'trapped' one where the pressure and emotional blackmail from her partner, along with a lot of mutual financial commitment added to her fear of the unknown with Rick. All made it too hard for her to take the risk of leaving.

Chapter 10

The Dance

"I love you, but I can't be with you now, but don't leave me"

In many cases, after very long periods of 'the dance' (that period where you know you are meant for each other, but one partner always finds reasons why they can't be with you just now but you mustn't walk away,) the 'solid' partner comes to the point where they can't take anymore and are forced to issue an ultimatum.

The 'runner' must then deal with the trauma of loss of the most important person in their lives, forcing them to look deep inside and get past the fears that have trapped them and us alike.

In my experience, there is nearly always a point where this is necessary for the 'solid' partner, as loving someone so deeply and not being able to be with them while staying in touch and being 'available' hurts so much, we come to a point where we can't pay that emotional price anymore.

Frequently, soul mate parting will trigger some degree of spiritual awakening—sometimes up to full awakening with the advent of visions and psychic awareness. Thus, we are bound to explore this and take our own internal journey of spiritual discovery. Seeking the answer 'why' will initiate this so that we might understand how our hearts know without any doubt that this person is for us, yet they have left and we remain with utter confusion, i.e. the head /heart split.

Along the way, we will begin to ask all sorts of questions about our direction and purpose and uncover things that we would have never realized had we not been forced into this position.

It is said the 'real' journey of life is the journey of development of the spirit to find how the path ahead lies on a more spiritual basis now that our lives have changed forever. Taking this path, we will frequently find that old ideas and passions and ways of living no longer hold the interest that they did, and many will look to psychics, religion and spiritualism for answers.

It is not uncommon for people to lose total interest in their job and other material things that were a part of their life prior to the awakening. The path is often extremely challenging as so much in our lives will change.

For a while, confusion reigns as we know that somehow deep down a change has taken place within us and that which made us content no longer seems to hold an interest.

Add this to the pain of loss and that's why losing a soul mate is the most traumatic experience imaginable. Hate, confusion and utter disbelief are common responses to separation. However, in order to help the karma along towards reconnecting, we will find that unconditional love and understanding towards our soul partner is the only way.

This can be unbelievably difficult in the first stages of separation, as the pain is so overwhelming we often fail to see how we can forgive someone for putting us through this. But as we continue along our path to awareness, eventually we find a place where the love for our partner is the only thing that matters and we offer them healing and forgiveness.

The quicker the two partners reach spiritual awareness and live out the karma, the quicker the reconnect. The link between the soul mates is an actual energy link. It's akin to having a twin, where this person feels part of us and part of our soul and indeed they are.

Q. So how do I make sense of all of this and my situation?

Sense is an intellectual function in the brain, Evaluating what is happening against other 'real' experiences and trying to find out what's going on. Words like obsession and phrases like 'Am I going mad?' flash through the mind in an attempt to compare this experience to others and find an understanding that will give us some peace.

The reason is that meeting a soul mate is a soul experience. It's an experience that is so unique it can't possibly be made sense of by comparing it to other more practical and every day things. The universe has decided that two people have to be together for a period of time and they are connected at a deep soul level. So, in fighting it, you are fighting the forces of destiny.

Make no mistake. When soul mates come together, there is a relationship beyond anything you will have experienced before. If you fight it or try to stay apart, the pain, anguish and confusion will show you just how special this bond is.

Lorna's reflections

Having thought through everything and analyzed it to death, I think I'm much closer to understanding things than the average layperson.

There were certain characteristics to the whole matter certainly, such as the incredible irony. If everything in the matter isn't just so ironic, then it probably isn't the true thing. The stages I found were something like what one goes through when someone dies. First, there's the incredible shock and realization that nothing can ever be the same again. Then there's the denial, no. can't be…didn't happen…wasn't me, whatever. Then there's the deep pain that hits so hard, and you carry for some time.

Then there's a kind of acceptance, and finally some sense of peace again. Also conversely, there are the stages of first love that everyone remembers from high school. First, the glow in the face and eyes is something that shines out of everyone, transcendental and ethereal, and makes everyone more attractive. Then they see with new eyes (rose-colored glasses) and see art and beauty in many things that weren't noticed before. Then you start to understand every poem, song or writing that delves around the subject of love. Then you realize that the depth of your feeling before, which you thought quite deep, was really shallow because there's miles below that which you've just struck into and that makes other relationships pale so strongly in comparison.

Physical reactions are varying. When embracing, you might feel a shift inside at the solar plexus like someone gently shoving you over saying, make room, we're finally together here, and you feel whole and more complete. I had struggles for most of my life over suicide. Once meeting that person, or realization of that person, even though the emotional strife is more than ever experienced before, I've had not one day of that struggle since, as the heart knows that once feeling the togetherness, it is inevitable that you must come together again. I've also had a strange golden patina to the light surrounding the circumstances, almost like a sepia tone, which told me in my heart that God was present or guiding me through these times.

The extreme physical reactions of heart flopping like a bass in a boat, the highs and lows, like Disneyland on drugs, all wrapped up in a big whirlwind that is hard to ride through.

The tsunami of love, 9.5 on the Richter scale of love, just short of absolute destruction. It is always bittersweet, antithesis and paradox, things and feelings together that just really shouldn't be, as they are opposites.

There is a great fear of the immense feeling because it is so hard to take, both the highs and lows. One always runs away or is taken away by a controlling person, because likely one partner always bends over backwards for people (so others can get a better aim to kick you in the head), and won't put themselves or their happiness as high as that of others. But there is still a communication on a deep level always present, that tells you that the other one is going through the same thing, and communicates the feelings and love back and forth that sustains through the rough periods.

And of course, you know that 'the surgeon has to cut deep for the healing to begin' and this always cuts the deepest, but is healed the quickest by the love of the partner.

Steve's Analysis

The observations offered here really give us an insight into the extremes of emotion and 'roller coaster' effect of a powerful soul connection. The whole experience is profound on every level and has twists and turns that test us every inch of the way.

Lorna's right in that she has made sense of the reason for the seemingly bizarre and that this is a process of extremes, a story of deep change, pain and healing leading to the ultimate love.

Chapter 11

Susanne's Story, Continued

He emailed on Friday after four of the worst days I've ever known.

I had been quiet…was everything ok?

I had meditated all week. What I heard from the universe was that I could have him if I wanted him. I just needed to be sure I wanted him. Of course I'm sure, I shouted back.

Damn, someone get a clue!

When I closed my eyes, I could see myself walking down my path and he would come and criss-cross it, until finally he joined me on the path, holding my hand. My relief at his email was exquisite. I tried to calm down. I could wait a month. Maybe the psychic was right. It wasn't personal.

In my next mediation, the universe was the one with the question. You know now that you care enough about this man to risk your own heart. But do you care enough about him to risk his?

Even I was surprised by the decisiveness and power of my response.

Damn right I did.

So I decided to take July off, have some fun, relax, let things take their course. I went to a spa for a week—spent a lot of time in the labyrinth trying to release him, but he wouldn't leave. I flew both my sister and my brother JD's seven-year-old daughter, the love of my life, into LA so we could all go to Disneyland.

They landed on Friday night, July 18th. Emma had 102 degrees of fever. Aunt and niece were both exhausted. We bought a thermometer, children's Tylenol, Popsicles, and called the landlady to come up and do the "mother test" on her. Was this just a high fever or was it emergency room material?

My landlady held her hot little hand to her cheek and assured us Emma would be fine. Around midnight, the fever broke and we had a slumber party. We drifted off to sleep, visions of Mickey Mouse in our heads.

At 4 am, my sister's cell phone ring. It was programmed with the "I Love Lucy" theme. I'll never be able to hear that music without flashing back to that night.

She missed the call. She checked the messages. It was Emma's mother, asking us to call.

"How did she sound?" I asked.

"Not good," my sister answered, but the line was busy.

Then, my home phone rang. 4 in the morning. 6 am in Texas. Something was horribly wrong.

I did a mental inventory. Emma was here. The voice on the other end of the phone was my father. They were my top two priorities. They were both safe. Part of me settled.

"Suze, JD is dead," my father said.

My sister says I dropped to the floor.

My brother, who was 40. Emma's father.

Telling a child that you love that her father is dead is the hardest thing I have ever done, or will ever do, in my life. I had broken the news to JD when our mother finally succumbed to cancer. I had listened to the two policemen at the door tell me my husband had been killed. This was harder. Part of me, as I sure part of her did, too, changed forever.

We all went back to Houston. My brother had not wanted Emma to come to California. I had dreamed the night before their arrival that he came to me and said she wasn't going to Disneyland. He was right.

I talked to Sheila the day of the funeral.

"Have you told Colin?" she asked.

"No."

"Well, I know he'll know exactly what to say."

She was right. He sent back a sympathetic and lengthy email that was concerned and thoughtful. As usual, he remembered things I had said to him in the past and repeated them almost verbatim back to me—one of the things I held on to as a sign he really cared. He asked me please not to hesitate to let him know if there was anything he could do.

At the time, I sincerely believed that he meant what he said.

Many of my Houston friends had their own problems. One's father died a few days before my brother. Another had a daughter in a difficult labor. Only one was able to come to the funeral, but she was there for me.

Back in LA, everyone was scattered. It was summertime. I was torn.

I desperately wanted to see Colin. If we were just friends, I would have called on him for comfort. Did I ignore my feelings and do so? Was using my brother's death as an excuse to expect him to be here for me the wrong thing to do? Would he only respond to me out of guilt and confuse me even more?

I decided on the first option. He had been a good correspondent, but I hadn't seen him in nearly a month. Joe was still gone.

I wrote on a Thursday and told him I knew he was on the new gym regimen, but the only thing my friends could do for me was to offer a little fun and diversion. I also said I would completely understand if he didn't have the time. I didn't realize then that he didn't have Internet access at home, or that he took Friday off from work. But, still, by 4 pm on Monday, I had not heard from him.

Every moment I waited had been excruciating.

So I fell back onto movies as an excuse—I wrote again, light and breezy and briefly, asking if he had caught any of the movies he had mentioned in last week's emails because

I was breathlessly waiting for reviews.

He wrote back promptly, within the hour. His email was 11 paragraphs long—hardly the response of someone who wanted to brush you off, I told myself. Yet not once did he refer to my request for fun and diversion.

I called a girlfriend again. Jenny said that, clearly, he was not interested in me, as a friend or otherwise, so wise up and move on.

I wrote back the next day, pretending everything was okay. We exchanged a few emails. I moved into forgiveness mode. But I didn't forget.

On the fourth day, unable to move past the hurt I felt, I wrote honestly to him.

Not in anger but as a friend would, i.e. my feelings were hurt and I wanted you to know because I don't think you wanted to intentionally hurt my feelings, particularly at a time like this, and we need to clear this up. I told him I was prepared that he might not have the time or inclination to offer me the fun or diversion I needed, but when he ignored my request completely, it had dealt a crushing blow for which I was unprepared. I could have handled a no, I told him, but I couldn't handle him acting as if I hadn't asked.

That was a Wednesday. Two nights later, I dreamed about him.

He lashed out at me—how dare I talk to him like that? And what did I expect, when I could sleep with anyone I wanted, how could he even think that I would want him? I tried to comfort him, but Emma's baby sister, Clara, was pulling on me, needing something.

I woke up. I had my answer.

By the time his reply came, I was in Texas again.

Emma's first day of school was looming, so the morning after the dream, a Saturday, the dog and I drove the 24 hours to Texas. The first thing Emma said to me when I told her JD was dead was, "Who's going to walk me to school?" I thought time on the road would give me a chance to process the pain and put it behind me and being there to walk Emma to school on the first day of second grade would show me what was important and what wasn't.

When his email came, the next Tuesday, I was babysitting for Clara, who was jumping on the bed while I struggled to open AOL on my brother's ancient computer.

His reply was blistering.

I never showed it to anyone, because it was the kind of response that girlfriends would have never forgiven and I didn't want anyone to hate him. I was ready for it, because of the dream, but it was still several hours before the blood left my face and returned to all the proper extremities.

Essentially, he said he assumed he would get over the way he had been treated, but that he thought we should wait for a quorum of the group before seeing each other. He said we could email about movies but he thought we should keep to that topic.

Again, I tried to process it—he wanted only a small part of me under extremely controlled conditions. Who and what did he think he was dealing with? Having a fight with your best friend is never easy, particularly when the best friend doesn't want to make up. I knew if we could just see each other, everything would be fine.

I had no idea it would be months of false stops and starts before I would have a chance to test the theory. I wasn't sure how I had gone from being injured party to being the accused, but conflict either ends a relationship or strengthens it. I wanted to get past this misunderstanding, much of which I blamed on the limitations of email communication.

Joe's month vacation turned into three. I left town for a two-week writing seminar. All I wanted, all I hoped for at that point, was to just get things back to where they had been. Just to have the friendship back. Slowly, our emails became less stilted and he did relax. Granted, we were both on guard. But his replies were prompt and lengthy and I was patient with the re-building process. I think he almost forgot about it.

The night we finally reconvened, in October, the old frequency was still there from the first sentence out of his mouth.

I had lost weight. I had a new hairdo and a new burgundy sweater. I had even had laser treatments on my skin, in that never-ending quest that seems required of women (particularly in LA) to look as young and pretty as possible. Colin saw me approach; Joe turned to greet me.

"Wow, you look great!" Joe said.

"How was SYLVIA?" Colin asked, knowing I'd seen a preview of the film with Gwyneth Paltrow earlier in the week.

"Gwyneth was wonderful, the movie was lush, but I didn't buy into the passion between the two of them and when that central love story doesn't grab you, the whole movie becomes a waste of time."

"How was the actor?"

"He was good, great even. I just didn't feel the chemistry."

"I've seen the husband, you know, and he's the kind of guy women go all gooey over."

"Seen him in person?"

"No, just on TV."

We were talking about Ted Hughes, the former poet laureate of Great Britain, and husband of Sylvia Plath, not the actor. Joe was clueless. He'd never heard of the poets or the movie. In exasperation, he waved his arms in front of our faces.

"What the hell are you two talking about?"

I realized then, whenever a third party joined us, there was an almost a physical separation required on both our parts, a re-tuning of the frequency if you will, so that others could tune into what we were saying. I saw the disconnect and the dial moving behind Colin's eyes, just as I felt the same emotions. We both did the sociable thing and tuned to a frequency that Joe could join us on.

It was almost physically painful to do so.

The evening was a start, but anticlimactic after the three-month wait. I knew now we could reconnect. The question remained, "Why?"

Again, the universe stepped up in unique ways and brought us together a few more times. We were back where we had been. But we weren't going any farther.

He left town for two weeks around Thanksgiving. The day he got back to the office, he wrote all of us and asked when we could get back together.

The last time I saw him was on December 12, 2003.

One of the things I had always liked about Colin was that he didn't shy from eye contact. On another evening where Joe didn't show, we had spent another four hours talking and I was sure now we were back on track.

That night, he didn't seem to fight the attraction. But on this last night, when he arrived at the tearoom where we were meeting for old time's sake, he had a hard time meeting my eye. (The screenwriter/psychic told me next day it was because he thought

I looked stunning and he didn't want me to know it and he knew I'd see it in his eyes.)

After a while, the three of us retired to a bar where I sat between him and Joe. Colin kept pressing his thigh against mine—and not taking it away—throughout the evening. This bar was louder than Friday's, so we kept having to press close. I could feel his breath on my cheek, almost taste him.

They walked me to my car later (something Colin always studiously avoided—he would walk me to my car after class and talk to the dog where she was waiting in the front seat, but *never* at the end of the evening). Colin's attitude was flippant—he was determined that he wasn't going to let me get to him.

Joe and I hugged goodbye, something that had started while Colin was out of town.

"What happened to handshakes?" Colin almost growled, offering me his hand.

I had an overwhelming feeling that I would never see him again.

To this day, almost nine months later, I haven't.

We kept writing, but his emails grew less personal, more distant. They were long and they were prompt, but they weren't going anywhere. I was searching endlessly for signs that he wanted me to go away. I never saw them.

Part of me wanted to see them, wanted to end the pain.

I had yet to learn that I was very ill and not getting enough oxygen to my brain and I was working a new job in an incredibly dysfunctional law office. A week or so had gone by where Joe and Colin and I were sending group emails back and forth. I would always send a shout-out to Colin on his cc when I responded to Joe.

But, at the end of January, four or five emails from Colin to Joe had come and gone, copied to me, and it was as if I didn't exist. Colin was not responding to anything I written to him, nor was he including me in what he wrote back to Joe. Also, an email directly from Colin to me that week had gone astray and he had misunderstood one of mine, causing him to become frustrated with me because of his misinterpretation!

An already tense situation was exacerbated.

So I wrote and asked if I was being oversensitive about being excluded or should I just take the hint? He wrote back that I was oversensitive, as usual, and what was it that made me think he was ignoring me?

I wrote back that his emails to Joe were very "guyish" and that I hated being treated like one of the guys when that wasn't what I was. He wrote back that he did not have "the time, energy or inclination to open that can of worms. Not to ignore you, but I'm going to the gym. Have a good evening."

As Sheila says, using a surfing metaphor, when it's time to jump, you know it.

The time had finally come.

So I wrote back:

"Colin—You've had my heart for a long time now, even if you haven't wanted it, and I've tried and tried to retrieve it on my own but without much success. I've wanted us to forge a true friendship, but perhaps I was wrong not to mention the elephant in the room so we can clear the air and get on with doing just that."

He wrote back later that evening. The email was in my inbox when I woke up. It was 2 pm that afternoon before

I found the courage to open it. Sheila called four times to find out what it said.

"I'm very sorry, Susanne. I wish there was something helpful I could say. I am probably the least likely source for that. To be clear, we will now have a long break. We cannot be great friends right now, because the elephant won't leave the room that easily."

I had known all along that I would be the one to lay my cards on the table. And, strangely enough, I had known Colin would kick my teeth in when I did. What I had never been able to see clearly was what would happen after that. Was holding hands on the path in my mediations a sign that we would be a couple or a sign that we would have an enduring friendship?

Usually, when a friend expresses a romantic interest that has no hope of being returned, they let you down easy and then try to be extra kind to you during the transition. If they value the friendship.

None of it made any sense.

But it did go on the back burner for a while, because I was in the emergency room within ten days, plagued by old health problems the medical establishment had told me I had to live with. When they nearly killed me, I got the attention of the doctors.

I was within 24 hours of death when I called Sheila and she did hero work getting me to the ER.

Most of February is a blur. I had two hospital stays, one minor surgical procedure, a second major surgery.

Sheila was there for me. Hadassah was there for me. Glenna was there for me. Even Joe, who actually sat with me the day I checked back in for the major surgery, waited until I came out of recovery and called my father and my sister after the doctor gave the word that I had pulled through. That's what friends do for each other.

Colin wasn't my friend. Ever. He never acted like a friend.

Yet he never acted like a lover, either.

I was pulled back from the brink of death for the third time in my life. Surely, there was still something here I needed to do.

Over the next few months, I doubted I would ever again see clearly and know why, though, because the loss and the hurt were the most overwhelming I had ever experienced. Nothing in my past prepared me in the slightest for the grief, hurt, disillusionment, confusion, and sheer physical and mental torture of this disconnection.

At this point, gentle reader, you may have the same mindset that well-meaning friends take. Clearly, he wasn't interested so what was it about this whole thing that I didn't understand? One thing I know for sure is that I have good instincts.

In my experience, men are the main thing that make women doubt those instincts. In my moments of clarity, I KNEW that he cared, too. I just couldn't understand why he handled the whole thing...or mishandled the whole thing...like he did. There had always been RESISTANCE...but there had never actually been rejection. Not in the sense we usually see it. Maybe that was the only thing I needed to know.

I've had more than my share of relationships. Once, when one was particularly painful, I had talked to a therapist. Her response was pretty much, damn, girl, you've had your share...what are you crabbing about?

I had always picked myself up by my bootstraps and gone on when the handwriting was on the wall. I didn't have blinders on...I'd bailed on three or four relationships in the past because I clearly was the one who cared and it was painfully apparent my intensity of feeling was not going to be returned, even though the men in question were tickled to keep me around as long as I wanted to stay on their terms.

I knew when a situation was unhealthy or had run its course.

I'd experienced intense connections with other men in the past, two of which blasted me out of long-term relationships. They were painful, yes, and full of life lessons, but they were clearly temporary and not meant to survive in the harsh light of day.

During the previous five or six years, I had reconnected with two former soul mates and had a closure with both which was fast and relatively painless…clearly, these relationships had not been meant to endure and I had let go of each graciously…and with a finality which was clear and unequivocal.

So why couldn't I put Colin in my past and move on to meet my future?

Not long after I got out of the hospital, I had a major epiphany about Colin. I had always been able to see the end of a relationship before…this guy was fun but not someone to share a life with, this guy was inappropriate but compelling, whatever. With Colin, I could not see the end of what we could be to each other.

The possibilities were infinite and seemed to stretch on and on. We could have so much together…and the only thing standing in the way of a phenomenal relationship was him. (As I write this, I wonder what his response to my side of the story might be, but this is my reality, regardless of how I impacted him. He was my teacher and this is the way I experienced these events and our connection, and I guess that's all that matters.)

I kept meditating; Colin invariably came into my mediations, usually filled with love and wanting to express it. I told myself not to glean false hope from this—on some level, we're all spirit and we all love each other and that could be what I was picking up.

I just couldn't understand his need to just cut me off. Nor could I accept it—and I needed either understanding or acceptance to find peace of mind.

I started calling psychics—my screenwriter friend said he would be coming back.

I called a new one.

She reassured me the feelings were mutual; he would come back. Most of the others I talked to said he was afraid of the intensity of his feelings; that he had problems with self-confidence; that he couldn't believe that someone like me could love him and if we started something, I would only discover who he really was and that wouldn't be enough, so why even start? I would only end up hurting him.

Trial and error uncovered several who were clearly reading the specifics of the situation—some amazingly so. Even the ones who said they didn't know why I would want him were willing to concede that there's no accounting for taste—and, yes, he was coming back!

When I finally discovered Steve, sometime in April, and read his theories on soul mates, it was as if someone was reading my mind—the mind I had been afraid I was losing! Finally, a heartfelt explanation and understanding of what I was experiencing every moment of every day—inability to focus on anything else, inability to find anything in my life which could bring me joy or comfort, a complete loss of interest in the things I'd found comfort in before, etc., etc.

He can explain it all so much better, and will throughout his book.

The road without communication from Colin has been long and hard—as I write this, it's been eight months.

I sent him a three-line email in May commenting on the lack of good films all year and asked if he'd seen anything worth recommending.

Silence.

Two weeks later, Joe admitted Colin had told him he didn't know what to say to me, so Joe suggested he just not write me at all. At one point after my surgery, Joe had told me everything I had done was out of love and kindness and I had nothing to berate myself for.

He said Colin had "issues" and did we really know of anyone he was truly close to? He didn't let people get close.

"He wants you, but he doesn't want you," was Joe's theory.

Well, at least his advice didn't cost $3.99/minute.

The middle of June, I wrote again, saying, "Hey, it's an old story. I expressed an interest, you drew a line in the sand, why is it impossible to believe that I'm a big girl who knows how to stay on her side of the line?" I also said I was giving myself permission to write to him anytime I had something to say.

Again, no response.

Giving myself permission to write him, though, kept me from doing it again. With the help and healing of advisors like Steve, I've regained a modicum of clarity and feel more like myself today than I have in more than a year, dating back to those first crossed-wires after my brother's funeral.

One advisor told me that every moment without your soul mate is an eternity. She was right. She was the same one who told me that his "resistance was futile." You can't fight the love of a soul mate.

For a long time, even though I knew the door was closed, I was hovering on the other side of it, waiting.

Now, I'm moving away from the mountain. Not because, like Alice, I want it to come to me. But because I have to live my life without the expectation of his return. Too many times, I felt him come so close, only to drop back again and make the choice not to contact me. Each time, it was as if I lost him all over again.

The practical part of me is choosing sanity. The other part just tries not to think about it.

Steve believes the return of a soul mate is inevitable—the karma has to be settled. I don't have to believe that anymore; even though, for a long time I did. I clung to that hope as if it were a life preserver. Yes, there's karma here. Maybe we won't have the chance to work it out—I won't ever understand that but I have an acceptance now I didn't have before.

Steve believes that when love doesn't bring your soul mate to you, the pain of your loss will eventually force them to reconnect. I hope he's right, but when I hear now from psychics that Colin will only come back as a friend (yes, they all say he's coming back…they just differ on why…will it just be for healing and resolution or will he actually want to stay?), I can handle it.

Finally, I can handle it if I never hear from him again. Life's possibilities are clear again.

I don't know why I had to go through this pain.

Sheila's theory is that I needed to have my heart opened up, to believe again in this kind of Love. She's said over and over that maybe it was just to open me up for the next man, the man who will stay.

She's the only friend who will tolerate hearing his name. She says it's not about him—it's about my process. She's my friend and that's what's important to her. The others don't understand and, maybe, they never will.

Finding others, like Steve, who have experienced the same love and loss has been one of my few comforts.

I want the universe to know that I'm ready to find someone to return my love.

I want someone who will step up to the plate and be here.

I want more than the starvation diet I've existed on since that January when I met Colin.

Being alone when there's no one special is hard enough; being alone when every moment is a separation from someone special is hell on earth.

It hasn't killed me, so I guess it's made me stronger. Like the chalice…just one of Steve's incredible analogies.

For a long time, I thought letting go meant my love wasn't strong enough so I was **so** stubborn about it…but I finally came to see letting go was the only way.

Coming through the gauntlet of fire and emerging on the other end, pure and fresh, unbowed and still standing with my heart fully open, is an amazing experience in itself...and, somehow, at this point, its own reward.

Chapter 12

'Runners'

As we said before in the example of the chalice, the heart needs to have developed to the level of being able to accept love and be completely free of pain and doubt in order that it can accept the ultimate spiritual love, that of a twin soul.

In many, if not all cases, one of the partners will be ready to accept this connection and the other not. From the majority of cases I've dealt with, the 'runner' usually has trouble accepting such a connection as it runs so deep and is so overwhelming that it affects them at a level where all of their past fears and pain lie.

Many, if not all, will have been deeply hurt before and have an underlying fear of relationships that are emotionally strong enough to hurt them, A lot will feel that luck in relationships has been so bad that they have problems believing someone anymore and that the situation they find themselves in is 'too good to be true.'

I frequently come across people who run from any emotions in their lives because they have deep and profound emotional issues from early childhood experiences that remain unresolved.

Generally, these people will vary from those that have been physically or mentally abused through to people who felt no parental love. All of these situations leave deep scars on otherwise beautiful, sensitive spirits.

Without exception, they are sensitive souls who feel deeply and therefore still suffer from this emotional pain, even though on the outside they may look perfectly happy and normal. In most situations, they can seem proficient and at ease; however, when it comes to something on an emotional basis, they will run and hide or often break down and not know how to deal with it.

A lot of these people are in relationships that they consider 'safe.' It will be apparent that there's no deep connection between the partners and, frequently, their partner may actually be very wrong for them and controlling and abusive on some level. It will also be apparent that they aren't happy; however, they seem to stay.

In fact, they trade a bad and oftentimes abusive relationship for taking a chance at a proper relationship simply because, if that person left them, they wouldn't hurt. To stay in a relationship that works practically but has no emotions means they feel safe, as they don't have to deal with their emotions on a day- to-day basis and thus avoid their buried fear and problems.

Many are trapped in relationships where they are controlled and their goodwill and good nature are used to keep them trapped, even though the relationship is dysfunctional. Usually the person will be subject to put-downs, blame and emotional blackmail which erodes their sense of worth so much they actually believe the person they are with is what they deserve, or that every problem in the relationship is their fault and they must try harder.

To the outside world, the abusive partner may appear to be a really nice partner but, behind closed doors, they will seek to alienate your soul mate's friends, use emotional tools such as blame and fear to put them down so much, they are scared to leave in case nobody else wants them, something they are often told.

Many will have a track record of running from a relationship as soon as it got too close and near to full commitment. This again is the total fear of having to dig deep into their hearts and knowing that commitment means dealing with the residual emotional insecurity, fear and pain.

Susanne's observation:

I was browsing the psychology books at the bookstore one day and came across a book on borderline personality disorder subtitled 'walking on eggshells.' I was struck suddenly by how that described my efforts to restore a semblance of a normal friendship with Colin after his failure to respond to my 'fun and diversion' email. After approximately six months of what I observed as fairly 'normal' behavior, Mr. Hyde had come out.

If I had seen such unusual behavior during those first few 'get-to-know-you' months, I might have been prepared, but there were no red flags. My inability to understand his behavior created much of the angst and hurt I suffered—had I done something horribly wrong? If so, please understand I didn't mean it and let's fix it!

On the night the handsome stranger talked to me, Colin had told a very revealing story. I don't remember how it came up, but he described an early childhood memory as if it were a scene from a movie.

His mother had put him and his sister in the car and left his father when he was six or seven. For a year, they hid from him—his mother was still in her teens when he was born and Colin hinted there were gambling and drinking issues (and there were hints later that he feared the apple hadn't fallen far from the tree!) After about a year, his father tracked them down.

He described his father kneeling on the front porch and looking through the mail slot, calling, "Colin! Colin."

"So you ran to him, right? I said, having worked as an attorney with abused children and observing over and over that it was normal for children to want to reconcile with a parent, no matter how bad the abuse.

"Oh, no," he said. "I knew we were hiding from him and so I ran up the stairs and locked myself in the bedroom."

My heart went out to that sensitive little boy, wrenched from his father, taught to hide from him. Later, the last night I saw Colin, we were discussing Christmas plans and I asked where his father was.

"London," he said.

"Do you speak to him?" I asked, trying to sound casual. He just looked away, shaking his head, then changed the subject.

The wounds of that little boy turned a bright, caring spirit into an emotionally maimed man. When I feel the 'soul pull' from Colin, and have to break away, it's because of the pain in my solar plexus. If I stay with it, it becomes a huge black hole, a pit almost, and I question if even the most unconditional gentle love could ever heal it.

Once, I asked a psychic to ask if he would let me go, release me from our karma.

"No," she answered. "You're here to teach him self-love. That's the agreement."

I would love to believe that's possible.

In all such cases, what affects our soul partners is that they do feel the connection very deeply and are good spirits but have been hurt deeply and or made to run from emotions at some point in their past. The fact that you are reaching a deep and lasting commitment can make them behave destructively toward the relationship, caused from a fear of the pain if it doesn't work.

This explains the sudden turnarounds experienced when they find reasons why they can't commit right now or they suddenly decide 'It won't work' for some reason. In a lot of cases, they will switch from "I love you" to "I don't love you," the fear of being hurt so powerful within them that they almost have to try and destroy the relationship but at the same time can't let you go.

Insecurity can play a major part in why your soul mate may not be ready to commit to something so deep and often they will project their insecurities, blaming you. I often hear people being told that their soul mate said they were the one with the problem as an excuse for not committing.

The truth is, they still have 'baggage' and fear and can't bring themselves to be sufficiently open about it, so they project it onto the partner.

In some cases, your mate may be with a controller who uses this insecurity to trap them in a relationship and so they're already with someone when you meet. The 'sixth sense' of the classic controller will find someone like your soul mate and seems to know they can use the person's caring side and their fear to trap them by devious means.

In other words, just as your spirit recognized your opposite spirit, so do dark spirits seek to control and own the light ones. The battle between light and dark isn't just in novels; it's here and now.

Many times, I find a soul mate will be trapped in one of these relationships where everyone can see it's bad for them but, for some reason, they stay.

This is their destiny—to have their eyes opened and to realize what's really happening and where they should be.

If your soul mate is in one of these relationships, the link between them and the dark soul can be very strong, but for the wrong reasons. They may have confused it with a soul mate connection, but in fact it's quite the opposite.

Upon meeting you, they will have suddenly been thrown into conflict as they have now experienced connections with both dark and light. It may take quite a lot of time for their eyes to be opened and, indeed, if they have been so badly controlled they may even confuse the two and see the one they are in as the right one.

Your task is to stay strong and know that now they have met you, their inner struggle has to be undertaken in order to find the right direction and come to a realization that the person they thought was good for them is, in fact, quite the opposite.

Ann observes:

"Soul Mate" relationships are a royal pain in the posterior. Wouldn't it be nice if all Clairvoyants could transmit past life history via telepathy, or other electric transmitters, to the sleeping counterpart/soul mate to wake their asses up? Don't suppose that would do any good either—then they'd most likely spend all their time locked in the loo!

Chapter 13

How the Connection Works

I've talked a lot about the spirit and the soul and the connection with your mate being at a deep and profound level. So how exactly does this work? Without going into detailed metaphysics, I hope the following explanation will show how some of the things you will be experiencing come about.

Our existence is well documented in physical and mental terms, i.e. we know about the body and the brain, but generally we know much less about the soul or spirit and what it actually is.
Simply, our spirit is our emotions, intuitions, fire, passion, character, senses and all that make us 'us.'

Conventional belief is that the brain is the center for most activity of sense, feeling and character; however, in actual fact, it is our spirit, an energy that resides in the body that makes us who we are.

Much of this traditional belief about the brain being the center of activity is because the brain and the body are three-dimensional objects which can be seen and touched and analyzed and therefore are more 'tangible' to scientists and physicians. Often we are told to "pull ourselves together" or "get over it" or "move on," as if our brainpower and self-will can control our emotions.

But try telling that to someone who's in love or in pain or who knows something in his or her heart that is undeniable. We don't feel love and pain in the brain, so how can we expect to suddenly change our emotions simply through thought and determination?

Ok, let's try an experiment...Just for a moment imagine someone you love and make yourself hate them...or imagine someone you don't like and make yourself love them...Well, I guess that proves our minds can't control emotions!

We can, of course, suppress emotions; we can squash them in like a car suspension spring in a box, but that doesn't make them go away and one day the lid is going to come off that box!

Much of my work as a healer focuses on suppressed emotions that have built up and caused the person life problems. Suppressed, unexpressed emotions are dangerous and damaging!

Lucy's story

My story is one that if a friend had told me she was in this position I would not have known how to react!! I am in love with a 19-year-old guy and have been for almost two years

I've been married for over 25 years and have never so much as "made eyes" at another man—although I can't say I have been deliriously happy in the marriage. I met this guy through my son of the same age and I had a very strong attraction to him from the first day I saw him two years ago. We are both very sensitive and artistic, although my artistic side I think has not been allowed to flourish throughout the marriage

There is just no age gap at all when it comes to our friendship— we get on so well, like we've always been together, like we've always been friends. The love is so powerful and painful that it physically hurts a lot. If I don't see him for a week or so, I am beside myself. The thing is, he is a teenager and needs to date and have fun…so I have to allow that to go ahead and that is quite difficult for me

There are many long looks between us and a mutual understanding that we love each other (in some strange way). The family have all picked up on the attraction between us despite me going to great lengths not to show it…both my husband and teenage children constantly make jibes about it, which is very unsettling!! We have been in each other's company out and someone has thought he was my husband! (Which is quite ridiculous give the age difference)…but obviously our closeness shows.

I have recently told him of my feelings for him, explaining that I love him overwhelmingly but I don't know what kind of love it is, I have never experienced it before. I said I didn't want to ever lose him as a friend and that I didn't necessarily want anything from him. When I am with him I feel complete, we laugh and have wonderful fun! I said perhaps I should stop phoning him but he suggested that if we tried to do that then the feelings would get more overpowering…although he admitted that he didn't feel as strongly as me he did not want to lose contact ever.

He also felt that the age difference was of no consequence. I dream of running away and traveling with my soul mate...but I am torn between my children's happiness and my own...and anyway would it ever be possible?

What has helped me a lot is writing poems/lyrics—it gets my feelings out so they are not bottled up inside—but their very existence is dangerous...as is our relationship!!

Q. Ok, so if we can't control emotions, how do they come about and how do they work?

Just as the brain processes information in a mechanical 'thinking' way similar to a computer, the heart processes information from which we 'feel' the effect.

Although the heart is the most obvious place where we are affected by change, there are six other energy centers in the body that also respond to external stimulus. These energy centers or 'chakras' define our senses, emotions, physical and spiritual well being and personality.

These energy centers house our spirit or soul...

So, in a soul connection, we are joined to our partner by some of these energies. Each of our seven energy centers is like a small radio transmitter and receiver, sending and receiving energy all the time. This is both how we sense and how we give out an aura to the outside world. In the case of a soul mate, we have met someone whose radio transmitters and receivers are on exactly the same channel!!!!

We use these senses every day to interact with people and places and yet we often do this without thinking. When viewing a new house, many of us will go on the 'feel.' "This is the right place, I just feel it!"

Likewise in a party, we will quickly and without thinking warm to some people and instinctively avoid others.

With a soul connection, we send out our signals and they come back on the same channel. Our radar is locked on to our partner and there's the instant Star Trek tractor beam scenario going on!

"Captain, all engines on full power, but there's noooo way we can fight it!"

And, just like the TV series, no phasers or shields will stop us being pulled into the beam.

Our soul and their soul recognize each other and have the "Where have you been since the last time we met thousand of years ago in a previous life?" conversation. And so we are hooked. This is the good news and the bad news!

This energy connection of the two spiritual 'radios' is what makes us realize this person is someone extremely special to us. As in any connection between two sources of energy, there is a flow of energy along the connection.

Jumper a flat car battery to a full one and the leads spark as a surge of electricity flows...

As in the laws of physics, where the power flows between batteries, the same applies to the laws of metaphysics. We connect to our soul partner and spiritual energy flows along that connection.

We link to them and they to us in a psychic/empathic way so that we can sense their emotions and they ours, whether they realize it or not.

Sometimes, when we aren't with them, the pain we feel will be utterly overwhelming, as will be the sense of total loss. We will also experience the 'soul mate pull' where we sometimes feel as if there's a rope around our heart trying to pull it out of our chest. Likewise, a dull pain may occur in the area just above the stomach and in the center of the forehead.

This, along with feeling 'lovesick' and sometimes heart fluttering and other seemingly random emotions, is a sure sign that our energies are being affected by our soul mate's energies.

THE BODY'S SPIRITUAL ENERGY CENTRES—'CHAKRAS'

CROWN CHAKRA: *Thought, Universal identity, oriented to self-knowledge*Related to consciousness as pure awareness. It is our connection to the greater world beyond, to a timeless, space less place of all knowing. When developed, this chakra brings us knowledge, wisdom, understanding, spiritual connection, and bliss.

THIRD EYE CHAKRA: *Light, Archetypal identity, oriented to self-reflection*Related to the act of seeing, both physically and intuitively. As such, it opens our psychic faculties and our understanding of archetypal levels. When healthy it allows us to see clearly, in effect, letting us "see the big picture."

THROAT CHAKRA: *Sound, Creative identity, oriented to self-expression*Related to communication and creativity. Here we experience the world symbolically through vibration, such as the vibration of sound representing language.

HEART CHAKRA: *Air, Social identity, oriented to self-acceptance* Related to love and is the integrator of opposites in the psyche: mind and body, male and female, persona and shadow, ego and unity. A healthy fourth chakra allows us to love deeply, feel compassion, have a deep sense of peace.

SOLAR PLEXUS CHAKRA: *Fire, Ego identity, oriented to self-definition*Rules our personal power, will, and autonomy, as well as our metabolism. When healthy, this chakra brings us energy, effectiveness, spontaneity, and non-dominating power.

SACRAL CHAKRA: *Water, Emotional identity, oriented to self-gratification*Related to the element water, and to emotions and sexuality. It connects us to others through feeling, desire, sensation, and movement. Ideally, this chakra brings us fluidity and grace, depth of feeling, sexual fulfillment, and the ability to accept change.

BASE CHAKRA:*Earth, Physical identity, oriented to self-preservation* Forms our foundation. It represents the element earth, and is therefore related to our sense of grounding and connection to our bodies and the physical plane. Ideally, this chakra brings us health, prosperity, security, and dynamic presence.

Three of these energy centers connect us to our soul partner:

THE THIRD EYE CHAKRA
Located in the center of the forehead, this is responsible for our psychic link, which allows us to sense the state of mind of our partner.

THE HEART CHAKRA
Connects our emotions and theirs; hence, the sudden and surprising emotional roller coaster effects as we feel emotions other than our own.

THE SACRAL CHAKRA
Located near the belly button, this is the power base of the connection where an invisible chord of energy ties us together.

Via these connections, our soul is connected or tied to that of our partner.

Often, we sense what they're feeling and thinking and when we're together, it feels like we're home, because the two souls are at peace together.

Being apart can be an extremely painful and difficult situation as the energies try to pull us to them. The 'soul mate pull,' as I call it, can feel as if your heart and a point just below the breastbone are literally being pulled.

When the relationship separates, the physical and emotional pain can be extreme as each party feels a loss similar to bereavement, as if we have lost part of ourselves. Remember, we aren't just feeling our pain, we are feeling theirs as well and that's what can make these situations extremely traumatic for those involved.

Love it or hate it, we're tied together via an invisible chord of energy, a 'golden thread' that binds our souls, our emotions, our lives, our mutual destiny. This is why a soul mate connection contains elements of both heaven and hell!

We can only marvel at the lessons we are to learn and the intensity of the emotions. Powerless in what lies ahead—the whole feeling of helplessness and hopelessness that overtakes us as we learn to surrender—our only option if we're going to live through it and learn our assigned lessons.

Chapter 14

The Box

Q. So, I accept that things will work out in time…How do I deal with it in the meantime and how can I have other relationships?

Don't try to move on unless you feel you're in a place where you can and can really believe that. Generally, we can for a time and then the realization floods back that we just can't 'get over' them.

You will be connected to this person and will love them until the situation resolves itself.

So put it in a box, place your love for them in a box in your mind and accept that wherever you go, it will always be there—but you are not going to allow it to stop you from leading a fulfilling life.

It's not a question of finding a replacement—don't even try.

Instead, demand your right to lead your life and have options. You may well not immediately find someone for whom you have the same depth of love—in fact, it's almost a certainty that you won't for some considerable time, if ever, BUT you can love someone on a conventional level and why shouldn't you!!!

Even if you aren't into the idea of finding love, get out and make friends and even date. By accepting that your connection will always be there but by removing it from blocking your path and carrying alongside, you give yourself permission to enjoy your life to the full whilst waiting for things to resolve.

I was discussing this box concept with my friend Helen. Having been through similar soul mate situations, we were talking about how to love people simultaneously but in different ways. She offers a very sweet analogy that I just had to mention. Her parents have a small dog and he is extremely attached to his toys. He knows the name of every single one and when asked to 'fetch Santa,' he dutifully returns clutching the Santa toy in his mouth.

Helen observed that even when he has a new toy he still loves the old ones just as much.

A simple but sweet analogy and very apt.

Using Psychics

A typical scenario I'm faced with in my daily work is where a person trapped in the waiting period of a soul mate connection has called a lot of psychics and been told by some that the person is returning and by others that they aren't

This variation has usually caused major emotional turmoil ranging from elation at the news of the imminent reappearance of the runner, down to massive depression when calling the next psychic just to hear that s/he wont return.

Yet both types of psychics offered very accurate insight into this person's life and was clearly picking up things they couldn't know so how could they vary on the question of the return of the soul mate???

There are several reasons for this variation…

Firstly, understand that being a psychic is a great responsibility and takes a lot of work. To stay highly attuned as a reader takes time and commitment so make sure to choose a reader who reads as an occupation. Remember that a reader's ability and experience vary greatly, so when you choose a psychic, choose carefully…Length of time of being a reader is not necessarily directly related to accuracy.

Always choose on the basis of the reader's customer feedback. See what other people say about them and take any headline statements of "99% accuracy" with a pinch of salt. In other words, always make your own mind up. A reading that feels right generally is right…trust your instincts.

So, to answer the question of how readers could agree on most things but be totally apart on the outcome of the $64,000 question—

Ok, the clue here is that we are dealing with a destined situation, something created, managed and controlled by the universe. We know this because of the immense strength of the bond we have, the unusual events and incredible emotions we have experienced.

In other words, we just somehow know that our situation is destined.

So, some readers may read you and your partner and realize that your runner can't or doesn't want to be with you right now, for whatever reason, and may simply project that fact forward as an outcome. But to read for a soul mate situation requires a reader to understand and have experience of karma and destined events. This is somewhat different from a 'regular' relationship reading as there are cosmic forces at work over and above the power of our free will.

The forces of karma are changing both of you and, ultimately, the situation.

Hence your reader is accurate on much of the detail but may not be reading the karmic energies and realizing that a reconnection has to happen. Reading a soul mate situation can require very special skills and experience.

Timing is always a hot issue within any discussion on psychic readings.

Take it from me that when a psychic is given timing on an event and reads it properly, it's usually correct. We are not given timings on a lot of situations and rarely, if ever, on soul mate relationships.

The world of spirit is mostly concerned with an 'order of events' controlled by karmic law.
Therefore, what will happen will happen when certain events have transpired to fulfill or settle the karma. We and our partner have to learn our karmic lesson and nothing will change until we

have. Think about it, how could the timing of this be destined even though the outcome is?

So when readers give you times, they are usually doing so to the best of their abilities. Realize that with a soul mate situation, it's nearly impossible to get the timing right as it is not pre- destined and therefore can't be read. I hear of many people being told they will be with their partner in June, then August, then March and so it goes on. Each time the person becomes more and more excited and full of expectation as they approach the appointed time, only to be deflated and demoralized as the time passes and nothing has changed.

Believe in the outcome, learn whatever lessons you need to be strong and have faith, and know that one day it will happen...

The main reason we seek readings when we're in this situation is that we have a massive conflict going on within us and are seeking understanding of seemingly crazy events and feelings.

Usually we have a knowledge, a feeling, a deep inner surety that this relationship is meant to be and isn't over. In fact, we are so sure of this that we fail to make sense of what's happening, i.e. our soul mate has gone and may have even said they aren't returning.

Hence the 'split.' Head says one thing and heart another.

What usually follows is a discussion with ourselves—something on the order of pulling ourselves together and realizing that we're kidding ourselves that they will return. We do the ' I just need to realize s/he's gone and stop being silly.'

However, what's deep inside doesn't change, that knowing that it isn't over…so we stay in conflict. In fact, we will stay in conflict until we realize that whatever we're being told, our soul or spirit knows the facts.

Try this test…

Imagine you have a million dollars. Try to make this as real as possible and think what it would be like to have that amount of money right in front of you now. Realize what it would mean to your lifestyle and visualize that.

So you have the money, now here's the bet—if you change your mind or bet on the wrong answer, you lose the lot.

You will have three seconds to place the bet.

Think carefully. Imagine that money in front of you. Make this as real as you can.

The question is, will you and your soul mate be together?

Now dig deep inside, use your instincts and **BET.**

If you managed to get into the scenario and really imagine the magnitude of the situation, you will have placed your bet on the knowledge of your deeper most instincts. This little experiment is to show you that there is an inner voice that does know the answer!

Q. So why have I experienced this relationship with all its pain and suffering?

Each of us lives our life on a different level of spiritual awareness.

A fairly sweeping statement, I agree, but what this means in practical terms is that some of us are old souls and some of us young souls—the old souls being more compassionate and giving and loving and the younger souls more material, self aware and less empathic.

Buddhists believe that we visit this earth in human form many times and each time our spirit returns, we (hopefully) learn our karmic lessons in order to transcend to the next spiritual level of existence— believing that only creating good karma, i.e. only having good thoughts and doing good deeds, allows our soul to ultimately transcend to the very highest level in as few lifetimes as possible and therefore not be required to return in human form again.

I guess the basis of this belief is that our time on earth is the time we are tested. And I don't think many of us would disagree with that, would we?

Buddhist or not, assuming we can accept that each person is existing on a different level of spirituality, we can understand why some of the phenomenon we experience only seems to happen to us as if we've been specially 'picked out.'

Ok, so what's a higher-level soul, I hear you ask?

An older or higher level soul is someone who is very aware of others, quite spiritual and interested in the meaning of life, nature and existence in general. They are creative, compassionate, kind, giving and caring, and have a tremendous capacity for love. This person's heart will make a lot of the decisions for them and they will view money and material possessions as less important than happiness and well-being.

In contrast, a lower level soul would be more self aware or selfish, less able to empathize or consider others and be very driven by material things such as money and power. Their capacity for emotion is sufficiently diminished that they would tend to lead their life and make their decisions based upon purely what they want rather than what they feel.

It takes a soul on a relatively high level to fully feel, sense and understand the connection in a soul mate relationship and to be freely able to wholeheartedly abandon themselves to it. Hence, soul mate connections happen to old souls.

So, if you're in one, it's a sure bet that you're an old and spiritually developed soul and you have already visited this earth in many previous forms, each time returning on a higher level as your lifetimes have been tasked with learning your karmic lessons.

The instant "don't we know each other" aspect of a soul mate connection comes from the two souls recognizing each other again as we have known these people in past lives but we didn't settle the karma. That is, we left that previous life with unfinished business between us.

And so we meet again...

The karma we left will manifest in some form or reason we can't be with our soul mate until each of us has settled our individual part of this past life debt. It may be that we are afraid of commitment, have been hurt in the past and don't want to go there again, or have decided what we want and aren't prepared to listen to our heart, for whatever reason. It may well be that we don't have sufficient self love to be able to properly abandon ourselves to the soul mate commitment until we have cleansed ourselves of all our pain and fear and are ready to fulfill our destined commitment to be together.

It is the duty of both partners to cleanse doubts and fear, remove wrong perceptions, heal and fully awaken to our destiny with our partner, after which we reunite to settle our mutual karmic debt and progress with out lives.

As I've said elsewhere, if the debt isn't cleared, it passes on to our next life and we don't reunite in the present; however, I firmly believe that the universe intends us to be together in this life and applies all the necessary pressures and synchronicity (coincidence) to force us to deal with our karma and come together in love and unity.

In other words, while there's life, there's hope.

Chapter 15

Surviving and Progressing

Techniques for mind, body and soul

All soul mate relationships involve the initial meeting and connection followed by the point where the connection is tested, usually involving a time apart with pain and confusion.

During this period, the two can't be together as each works on dealing with personal karma until each is totally free and clear and able and ready to fully accept the relationship on the deepest spiritual level.

The most common situation I come across is that the 'runner' NEEDS to stay connected with you as a friend or to keep contact, but without committing to a relationship. This just maintains the 'dance.' They don't want to lose you from their life but, for the solid partner, life becomes a roller coaster of hope and disappointment, of love and pain.

Messages are often contradicting, the most extreme being 'I love you', and then a week later 'I don't love you.' Or 'We will be together,' then 'We can't be together.'

Seemingly normal people who love us behave as if they're going out of their way to hurt us and *it makes no sense*. The dynamic behind this is that the power of the link throws them into total turmoil. By staying in contact during this period, we get thrown around with them like a cork in a storm.

Usually, there comes a point where self-protection is vital and we must detach in order to save our sanity and regain some emotional peace, albeit at a very high cost—by pushing our soul mate away. Karma can only be fulfilled as each of us individually deal with the connection and find our own answers whilst we are apart.

Once we have detached and have decided to work on our own survival and strength, there comes healing and waiting. Healing to put us back together and get emotionally, spiritually and physically back to 'normal,' and waiting to see what happens next and when.

After separation, we can find it impossible to 'move on' and to get our mate out of our heart and out of our mind. The experience can be the most traumatic we will ever experience. Often, we are so traumatized we can't work or eat or sleep. Grieving as if we have lost someone close is very common, as is depression and living on our nerves.

Emotions are a roller coaster as Lorna describes so well...

"The extreme physical reactions of heart flopping like a bass in a boat, the highs and lows, like Disneyland on drugs, all wrapped up in a big whirlwind that is hard to ride through. The tsunami of love, 9.5 on the Richter scale of love, just short of absolute destruction. It is always bittersweet, antithesis and paradox, things and feelings together that just really shouldn't be, as they are opposites."

Inside, we somehow know that this person isn't gone from our lives, yet to all intents and purposes it seems that they have.

In order to understand what's happening here, we must appreciate that this is a process, a tunnel we are being forced through in order to emerge in a different place in our lives. We are both being 'forced' by the universe to live out our karma until we can be together again.

So the golden rule is to live it. However hard, however painful, we have little choice but to know that whatever is happening is happening for a reason.

We may blame them, ourselves, the universe…we may think 'why me, what did I do wrong??'
The fact is, nothing! If you're having a soul mate experience, your soul is about to transcend a level of existence.

Okay, so now you're saying: 'But I don't want to!!!!'

As you have undoubtedly realized, you have little or no choice in the matter. The forces at work here are beyond our control. But think about it, maybe they need to be. Who in their right mind would wish to go through such a traumatic experience even if we knew at the other end lay our ultimate happiness?

I believe there are times when destiny takes control and all we can do is roll with it.

During this period of time, there are many techniques to help us heal and to help us gain clarity on what has happened, is happening and will happen.

The Mind—Understanding and Acceptance

If you have had the experiences, feelings, situations or symptoms we've described throughout the book, realize that you aren't 'imagining' this. You are connected with someone at a spiritual level and you don't have any choice about that.

Why ? For better or for worse, the connection has been made. Understand that the connection is for a reason, although right now you may not know that reason.

What ? It may feel as if your whole life is changing and suddenly you're thrust into a new surreal situation where everything that was once under control seems in chaos. I remember feeling like 'This isn't my life!' Believe that these enormous changes are necessary and don't lose hope that things will settle again

Contact. If you haven't been able to resolve your situation yet and they won't or can't meet your needs, then stay clear until they can. Don't put yourself in a position where you can be further hurt and frustrated. However much you fear losing them, focus on healing yourself first.

Destiny will have her way—there is nothing you can do to change destiny, so stop questioning why. The strength of the experiences and emotions you are going through are showing you that there are powers at work beyond your control, so welcome those powers and try to stay positive about the outcome.

Commit to heal and to improve your situation. Be selfish for a while and be determined to get through to better times.

Regret is a negative thought/emotional response and inhibits healing. Nobody can change the past, so eliminating regret is an important first step to begin healing

Anger is a natural emotion, albeit a destructive one. When you feel anger, try to accept the situation and dispel the anger. Don't be mad at yourself.

Don't blame yourself or others, the situation exists and that's a fact. Blame just creates more negativity and confusion.

As someone once said to me, "Destiny has bought you this far—do you think she's going to drop you now?" There is a reason for your experiences and that reason is to get you to a better place in your life. Nothing happens by accident and the universe isn't just cruel.

My research shows that most people going through painful soul connections will consult a psychic and many become dependant on psychic readings, to the point of spending large amounts of money that would otherwise be considered outrageous. This often leads to feelings of guilt and panic.

As well as needing constant assurance throughout the pain of soul mate separation, one of the reasons for contacting psychics more than 'usual' is that most psychic's healing energy temporarily allays the pain.

A more effective (and certainly more cost effective) way to deal with this is to find a spiritual healer and undergo Reiki or other such energy healing.

My website www.naturalenergytherapy.com explains the NET (natural energy therapy) techniques I have developed for soul mate connections, which are proven to be fast and extremely effective. This healing works remotely as well as in a one-to-one situation. If you would like to learn the techniques or your healer wishes to find out more, please see details on the site.

In all cases, if in any doubt, consult a medical professional. Make sure your counselor has experience of soul mate trauma.

Don't fight it—once we stop fighting it, the healing begins.
As Johnette observed about her situation—in fighting her destiny she was "boxing with God but her arms weren't long enough."

Negative thought patterns, behavior, beliefs, people and situations.

There is some sort of cosmic rule that guarantees someone will say to you things like "Pull yourself together," or "S/he wasn't worth you" or "There are plenty more out there."

Try and understand that often people won't understand or have experience of the depth and extreme nature of a soul connection and will feel helpless to assist you. Therefore, allow them their clichés and see that they are just trying to help.

It is common to want to leap into another relationship to 'get over this one' or to indulge in some forms of excess or destructive behavior when caught in extremely painful and debilitating situations.

This behavior just avoids dealing with the emotions and delays healing. It can also lead to guilt and remorse when the destructive phase ends. If in any doubt, always consult a physician or other medical practitioner.

Reiki and other such spiritual healing methods are most effective at dealing with soul pain as they work on the same spiritual energy level as the soul mate link itself.

Talk to your practitioner or see www.natruralenergytherapy.com for advice and guidance on the proven NET healing techniques.

Use whatever safe and sensible means you need to take your attention off the pain and confusion from time to time. However, on a long-term basis, you need to express your emotion and pain in order to heal so use diversions only when you have to.

As Winston Churchill said, "If you're going through hell—keep going!"

Don't wait—act. Focus on yourself and your life and be determined to heal and move toward better times. Demand your right to happiness and work towards it.

Allow yourself time to heal and take one day at a time. Each day is one day closer to happiness and a resolution.

Karma is at work here. The universal law of balance must be obeyed. So if you've been through hell, then trust that karma needs to redress that pain and suffering with love and happiness in the future.

Don't focus too much on the future and the outcome. Focus on improving each day in your life knowing that pain and confusion must and will pass.

The Body—Feeling Better

Some of the symptoms of the interchange of spiritual energy between soul mates are shivers down the back, occasional heart 'flutter,' a tugging feeling below the breastbone, feeling hot or cold and sudden waves of emotion and anxiety.

Always consult a medical professional when experiencing abnormal physical conditions

Sleep patterns can be the first thing to suffer. Excessive worrying about lack of sleep can exacerbate the situation. Talk to your doctor and also consider herbal sleep aids.

Baths and warm drinks can help sleep. Also, consider burning incense as a relaxant.

I found massage a great help to relax and relieve physical tension. Aromatherapy massage is particularly effective.

Ben & Jerry should be given an award for their contribution to spiritual healing! A good DVD and some comfort food (in moderation and subject to your diet, of course) can help relaxation. Swimming, saunas and Jacuzzis are another treat that help relax the body.

Panic attacks and waves of emotions seemingly coming from nowhere are commonplace when going through extreme trauma.

Emotions are meant to be felt and not bottled up so, however difficult, try to express them and not fight them.

As the pain and loss are expressed through emotions, such as crying, it releases the pain. Try not to fight it.

Bear in mind that, as you are connected to your soul partner, you will also feel their emotions. This can be very confusing. For instance, you may be feeling fine and then all of a sudden sense an emotion that doesn't seem to be yours. In this case, visualize 'pushing' that emotion away and you will find it allays the symptoms.

The Soul—Dealing with the connection

The main symptoms of being spiritually connected but not physically together are: confusion, pain, and an immense sense of loss similar to bereavement. Feeling in a sort of surreal state (detached from reality) is also common, as is sensing your soul mate around you very strongly, which adds to the confusion.

What we're dealing with here is two souls connected across time and space by the Universal Life Force Energies—meaning the basis of what you are experiencing is founded at an energy level, the stuff that our souls are made of. An energy that connects us to the rest of the universe—it's what psychics read and healers manipulate.

Yes, it does sound like something a man with a white beard calling himself 'Dark Raven' would be twittering on about, but if you're not sure about how real unseen energies are, just go over to the TV set and find where the radio waves come in. Grab a few and post them to me.

What do you mean, you can't! They must be real, mustn't they, because there's a picture on the tube?

And if you still aren't sure about cosmic 'soul' energy, consider this—nothing else makes sense of the situations we describe here except for the presence of that force. That force which connects us to our soul mate across space and time. Aren't you already feeling its power??

So let's do away with the 'pulling ourselves together' and 'moving on' and all the other clichés that are as relevant as a bottle of carrots.

Meditation—a way to peace

Sounds difficult to do, doesn't it?

Well, the secret to meditation is that it puts us back in direct touch with out soul, our inner energies and brings rapid peace and a feeling of wellness. It's MASSIVELY beneficial in soul mate situations and it's REALLY easy to achieve.

Meditation is the direct way to access the energies that link us to our soul mate and therefore once we can enter the meditative state we can settle our emotions and find peace.

Ok, so here's how we do it...

Find a warm, quiet, comfortable, dimly lit place and settle into a relaxed position. Make sure legs and arms are uncrossed and nothing is drawing your attention from the meditation. If you like, light a candle and burn incense, as this helps.

Gentle meditation music or just any relaxing music without lyrics also helps.

Forget what you may have heard about emptying your mind or focusing on waves or clouds or chanting mantras or any of the modern myths about meditation.

Close your eyes and simply imagine feeling the warmth of the sun on your skin as you relax.

The fact that we are linked to our partner by a spiritual energy means that by default we have a 'psychic' connection with them. This link is responsible for much of the roller coaster emotions and other phenomenon we experience as energy travels between the two souls; however, we can use this link to our advantage.

If, for example, we want to find out how they are feeling or what they are thinking, try the following:

Sit with your eyes closed and imagine your soul mate sitting opposite you and looking into your eyes. You may be surprised by what you sense! This is a well-proven technique so give it a try.

Surprising as it may seem, we can manipulate the energies we send and receive along our spiritual connection.

The following technique is singularly the most effective technique for dealing with times when we feel stressed and emotionally drained and pulled by the energy—the soul mate 'pull.'

Close your eyes and simply visualize your soul mate standing ten feet from you. Don't worry, it doesn't have to be a convincing visualization; just their outline or any representation of them will suffice.

Now, imagine building a wall between you made of rose quartz crystal. Make it as high and as wide as you like, but build the wall in any way you can easily visualize. As the wall grows, make it deeper and deeper between you so that the image of your mate is pushed backwards by the wall. Keep on going and you will find that your emotions settle and you feel calm almost immediately.

Although it isn't obvious why this works to those who aren't initiated into energy work, the visualization process changes the energies between us and calms them to alleviate difficult emotions and strain. This really does work!!!

Writing down how we feel, including all the pain and anxiety we've been through, is a very therapeutic process. Not only does it allow us to express emotions we may not be able to express directly to the person who caused us that pain, it also helps find clarity and release.

The writing process can be very emotional as we relive painful events and memories however this is essential to release the unexpressed feelings and set ourselves free.

Write your letter as if addressed to your soul mate and express every feeling and thought.

Finally, forgive them for what they did to you. This can be the most difficult thing of all, but the potential for cleansing and emotional release is unparalleled if you can manage to achieve this.

Take your letter outside and place it in a container where it can be safely burned. Some people choose to tie a red ribbon around the letter and make the burning more of a ritual.

Say to yourself and the universe that you set these emotions free, and burn the letter. Watch the smoke rise and realize that you are releasing yourself free from pain as the smoke dissipates up into the sky.

Practitioners of spiritual healing arts such as Reiki or crystal healing area are godsend to those suffering soul mate pain.

Healers will work with your energy and rebalance you to help alleviate pain and suffering and release destructive emotions.

Chapter 16

I Found My Soul Mate

Andrea's story: My first encounter with Nigel was at school when someone pushed me during a fire practise and I fell over and broke my ankle. An older boy with bright eyes, curly blonde hair and a cheeky grin came along and asked if I was okay. This was Nigel. He was just leaving school and I was in my first year so after that we didn't really talk or see each other.

Later, at the age of seventeen, I was a rebellious punk who was into Supertramp. I was not getting on with my parents and it's fair to say I had issues. But my Nan looked after me like a mother and I worshipped her. We lived in a small but pretty village in the Cotswolds where I had lots of friends, young and old, particularly Mel, a girl I met in secondary school, who was also unconventional.

Nigel was now 21 and popular with the ladies although, like me, he was unconventional and rebellious. I think this was because he was forced to be self sufficient from the age of twelve, since his childhood wasn't a pleasant time due to his father being a bully and a control freak. Nigel lived in a pretty village five miles from me and had just proposed to a local girl and was soon to be married.

I was with Mel in the village social club, near the toilets, when we ran into Nigel.

We said hello and Mel said to him, "I heard that you're getting married—that won't last!"

At that point I headed off to the loo, as Nigel's last words were, "We'll see." As I turned my head to look back, he caught my eye. I saw his sparkly eyes and blonde curly hair and that naughty boy smile and from that moment, I knew him. I walked off smiling, as I knew something had opened up between us, and I needed to leave it. But, somehow, I knew he would be there for me in the future.

As the years went by, I saw Nigel occasionally when we passed in the street. By now, I had three children and Nigel had four and one day one of mine and one of his mixed up their coats at school so we later exchanged them at Nigel's house. As I went to his house and saw him again, that same recognition was there, as if I knew him and we would meet again.

Later, I decided to place an advertisement in the lonely-hearts column. I didn't know until years that Nigel saw it and decided to call. He even asked my son, who was a friend of his son's, what he thought about it, not realising it was me. But, in the end, he didn't call.

In 2001, I was single and a mother of three and Nigel was a widow and father of four who had just returned from a holiday in Greece and was looking good. We met again at the supermarket and he made a point of saying hello. After he walked away, my friend commented on how nice he was but not my type! Later, I learnt his daughter asked who I was and said I was nice and he agreed! In March 2002, I was in my garden covered in mud and looking forward to a nice hot bath when my friend Terri popped her head round the gate. Terri had just split up with her boyfriend and wanted a night out. I wasn't all that interested, but Terri twisted my arm.At the nightclub, Terri abandoned me as usual and I needed to escape some lounge lizard of thirty, a desperado whose wife didn't understand him. I needed an excuse so I decided to go to the toilet and make good my escape.

As I emerged from the ladies toilet, dressed in red trousers and a black frilly shirt, still unconventional to a point, I scanned the club. The music cut and it was silent and, although I wasn't aware of anyone else around me, through the smoky haze I saw a familiar face, a blast from the past.

Ahhhh, I thought, oooh it's Nigel, and on I marched over to where he was propped against a pillar, dressed in an unusual jacket, thinking that he was still just as lovely as I remembered him 21 years ago when I went into the toilet.

But now I knew what to say, as I had found him again at last. I knew he was waiting for me! He leaned over and kissed me, but his wife's sister saw us and didn't like him kissing someone, as his wife had died just eighteen months before. So out meeting was interrupted.

Later that night I went with Terri to the twenty-four hour café and he was there!!! Later he told me he was sitting there praying I would walk in. He had found me and he didn't want to lose me again. We sat and drank hot chocolate like it had always been this way. He is me and I know he's mine and he's meant to be mine. We have been together ever since.

I have found my soul mate, I feel as though I have come home. Spiritually I am no longer alone. No more darkness no more loneliness a true life long mate who I have found at last.

Steve Comments;

This what it's all about; that glorious Technicolor moment of joyous defeat, when the walls go down and fear flies out the window, when each soul mate surrenders to the other. The moment when Harry rushes to find Sally, when Meg Ryan risks it all to go to the top of the Empire State Building and meet Tom Hanks.

Cue end music
Fade to sunset

Chapter 17

Something to Ponder

I found these quotes inspiring on my journey and hope you will too.

I believe all suffering is caused by ignorance. People inflict pain on others in the selfish pursuit of their happiness or satisfaction. Yet true happiness comes from a sense of peace and contentment, which in turn must be achieved through the cultivation of altruism, of love and compassion, and elimination of ignorance, selfishness, and greed.—Dalai Lama

Old friends pass away, new friends appear. It is just like the days. An old day passes, a new day arrives. The important thing is to make it meaningful: a meaningful friend—or a meaningful day—Dalai Lama.

Don't be afraid of showing affection. Be warm and tender, thoughtful and affectionate. Men are more helped by sympathy than by service. Love is more than money, and a kind word will give more pleasure than a present—Jean Baptiste Lacordaire

Don't judge each day by the harvest you reap, but by the seeds you plant.—Robert Louis Stevenson

Finish each day and be done with it. You have done what you could; some blunders and absurdities have crept in; forget them as soon as you can. Tomorrow is a new day; you shall begin it serenely and with too high a spirit to be encumbered with your old nonsense.—Ralph Waldo Emerson

Man's reach should exceed his grasp, or what's a heaven for?—Robert Browning

Keep away from people who try to belittle your ambitions. Small people always do that, but the really great ones make you feel that you too, can become great.—Mark Twain

When you reach for the stars, you may not quite get them, but you won't come up with a handful of mud either.—Leo Burnett

The future belongs to those who believe in the beauty of their dreams.—Eleanor Roosevelt

And finally something especially relevant to our book...

If you're going through hell, keep going!—Sir Winston Churchill

Remember that when soul mates finally reunite it is the most unbelievable relationship. Even if it's meant to be a transient one and not the ultimate lifetime connection, the reconnecting is an amazing experience and worth whatever price we had to pay on the way.

Good luck on your journey.

Printed in the United Kingdom
by Lightning Source UK Ltd.
130088UK00001B/106/A